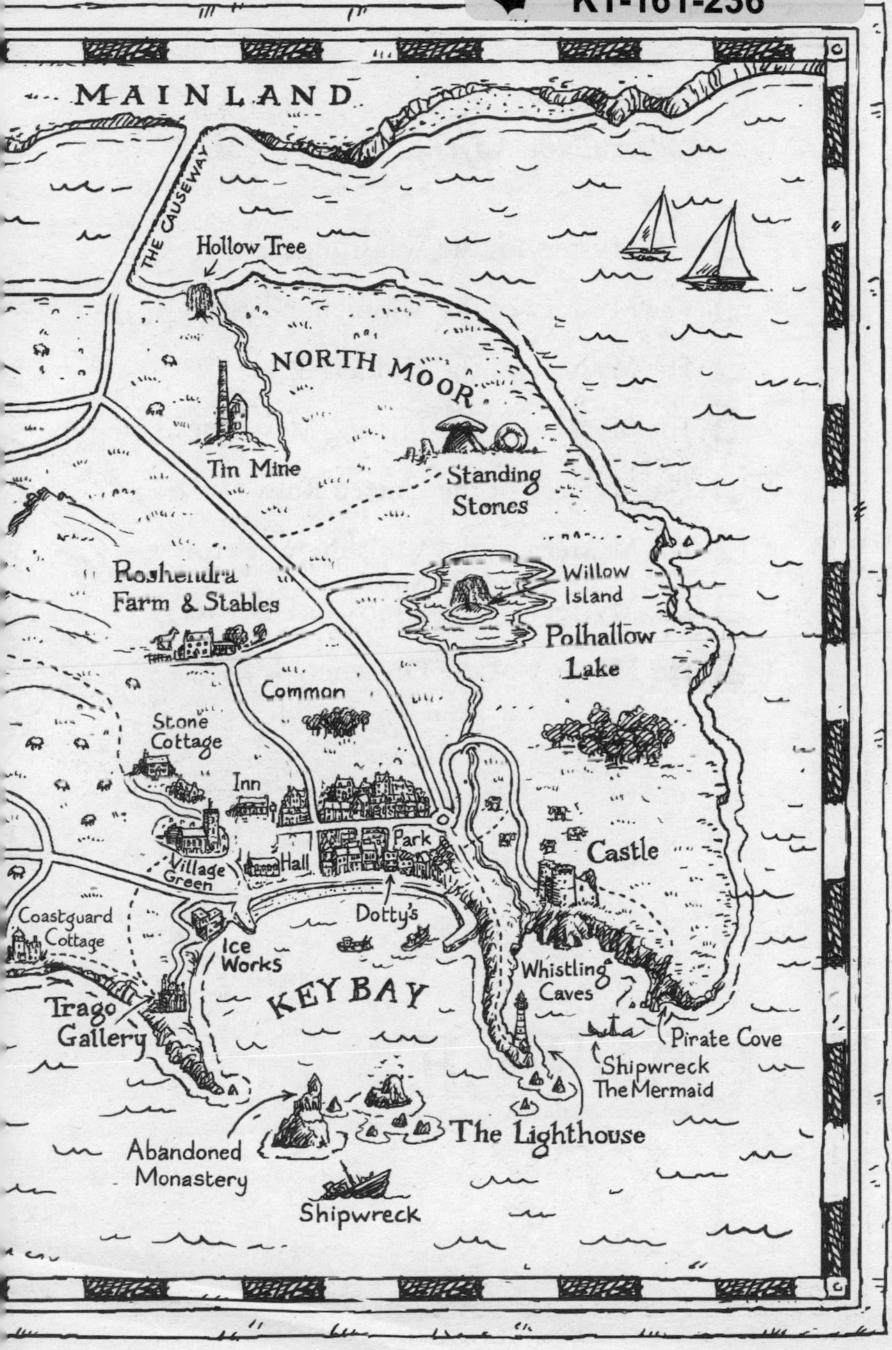

MAINLAND
THE CAUSEWAY
Hollow Tree
NORTH MOOR
Tin Mine
Standing Stones
Roshendra Farm & Stables
Willow Island
Polhallow Lake
Common
Stone Cottage
Inn
Park
Castle
Village Green
Hall
Dotty's
Coastguard Cottage
Ice Works
KEY BAY
Whistling Caves
Trago Gallery
Pirate Cove
Shipwreck The Mermaid
The Lighthouse
Abandoned Monastery
Shipwreck

Collect all the Adventure Island *books*

- ❑ The Mystery of the Whistling Caves
- ❑ The Mystery of the Midnight Ghost
- ❑ The Mystery of the Hidden Gold
- ❑ The Mystery of the Missing Masterpiece
- ❑ The Mystery of the Cursed Ruby
- ❑ The Mystery of the Vanishing Skeleton
- ❑ The Mystery of the Dinosaur Discovery
- ☑ The Mystery of the Drowning Man

ADVENTURE ISLAND

THE MYSTERY OF THE DROWNING MAN

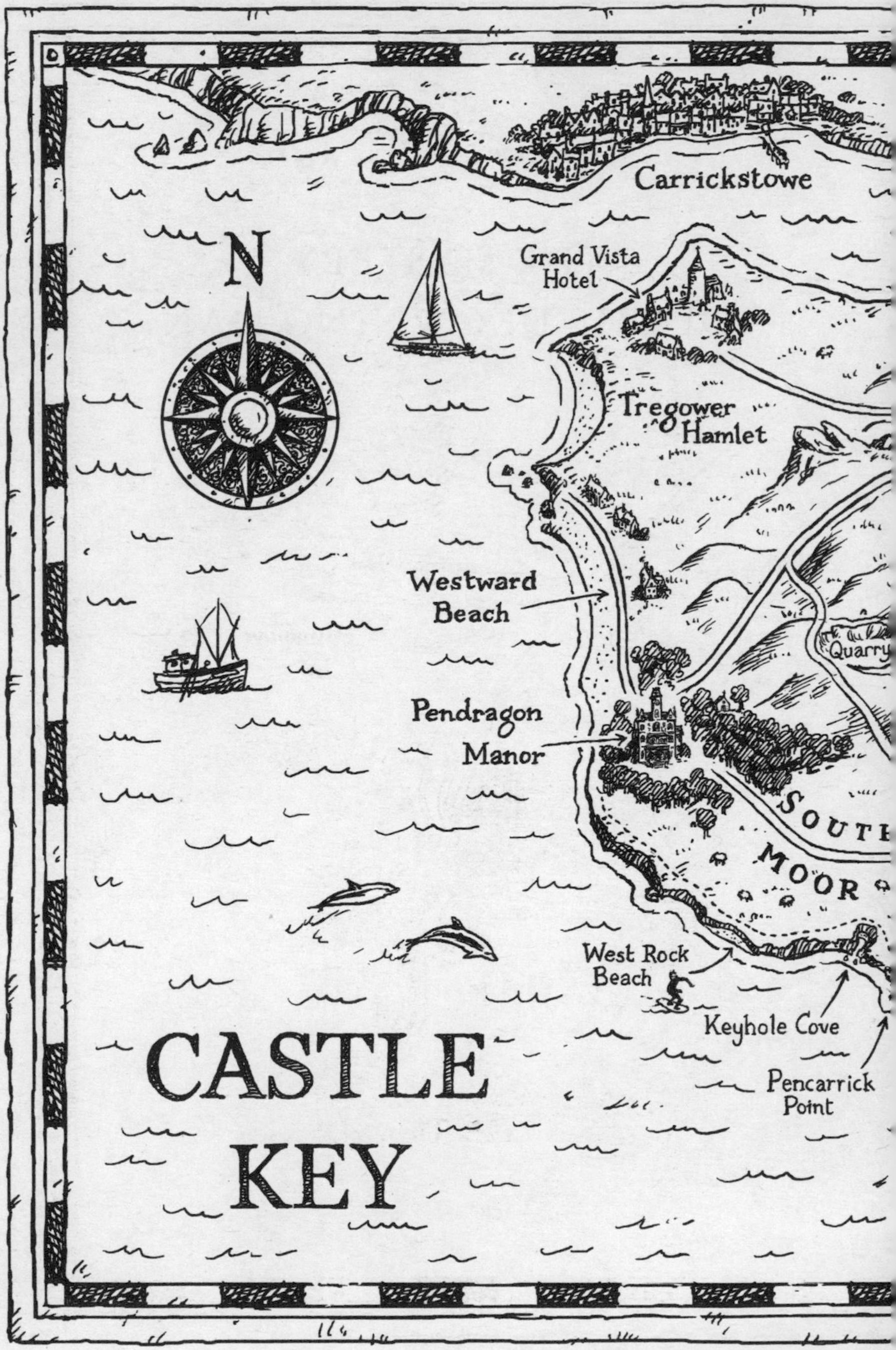

Carrickstowe

N

Grand Vista Hotel

Tregower Hamlet

Westward Beach

Quarry

Pendragon Manor

SOUTH

MOOR

West Rock Beach

Keyhole Cove

Pencarrick Point

CASTLE KEY

Helen Moss

Illustrated by Leo Hartas

Orion
Children's Books

First published in Great Britain in 2012
by Orion Children's Books
a division of the Orion Publishing Group Ltd
Orion House
5 Upper St Martin's Lane
London WC2H 9EA
An Hachette UK company

The Orion Publishing Group's policy is to use papers
that are natural, renewable and recyclable products and made
from wood grown in sustainable forests. The logging and
manufacturing processes are expected to conform to
the environmental regulations of the country of origin.

A catalogue record for this book is
available from the British Library.

Printed in Great Britain by Clays Ltd, St Ives plc

For my friends, for support and sanity

One

Out of the Blue

Emily Wild lay on her stomach on the warm rock, her head propped up on her elbows, and gazed across the water towards the gap in the cliffs that circled Keyhole Cove, almost cutting it off from the open sea. The hidden cove on the south coast of Castle Key, guarded by a battalion of jagged rocks, was once the haunt of smugglers running brandy and tobacco to Cornwall. Now it was one of Emily's favourite places on the island.

It was the first day of the Easter holidays. Her friends Scott and Jack Carter were back from London to stay with their Great-aunt Kate. Together they'd rowed Emily's little boat *Gemini* all the way to the cove and had spent the morning swimming and exploring rock pools, before stopping to eat their picnic. Sunlight was sparkling off waves of the deepest blue.

Everything was perfect.

And yet . . .

Emily's little dog Drift nudged her chin with his nose. He could tell something was troubling her.

She scooped up a handful of the tiny shells that sprinkled the beach like silver glitter, let them run through her fingers, and sighed. 'I hope we don't get any mysteries to solve this holiday!'

Jack was so shocked he dropped his ham roll. The girl lounging on the rock next to him *looked* like Emily Wild: the same mad tangle of chocolate-coloured curls, the same dark eyes, the same skinny brown arms and legs. And yet, this *couldn't* be Emily. Emily *lived* for mysteries! Her pen was permanently poised over her notebook, itching to write *OPERATION X* (with a double underline, of course) and a long list of suspects.

Either this girl was an imposter or something was seriously wrong.

Scott clearly felt the same way. 'What are you on about, Em?' He glanced up from under his floppy fringe. 'You're not *ill*, are you?'

No way! Jack thought. *Emily* couldn't be ill. She was as tough as those wild grasses that sprouted from the sand dunes.

Emily laughed. 'Of course not! It's just this stupid music festival Dad's organizing up at the castle. From tomorrow I have to help Mum with cleaning and cooking every day because we'll have loads of guests at The Lighthouse and Dad'll be so busy. Even if the crime of the century was committed right under my nose, I wouldn't have time to investigate . . .'

Relieved that Emily wasn't suffering from some obscure disease, Jack salvaged his roll and brushed off the sand. He stuffed one half in his mouth and threw the other in the air. Drift caught it neatly in his jaws. 'Is that all?' he laughed.

'We'll help with your jobs,' Scott offered.

Jack nodded in agreement – although secretly he planned to leave the helping-with-jobs part to his brother. It was Scott's idea, after all, and this *was* meant to be a holiday. 'I bet Sherlock Holmes didn't have this problem,' he laughed. 'Sorry, Watson, old chap, you'll have to crack the case of the Hound of the Baskervilles on your own because I've got to polish the toilet paper.'

Emily grinned. 'Thanks, guys!' Scott and Jack could be infuriating at times, but they were the best friends she'd ever had – apart from Drift, of course! Recruiting them onto her investigations team when they'd first come to stay in Castle Key last summer had been one of her smartest moves ever. 'Not that I'm expecting a major case to suddenly pop up out of the blue,' she added, 'but you never know!'

'And anyway,' Scott said, watching Drift chase a crab into a rock pool, 'your dad's festival isn't stupid. It's cool. He's got some awesome bands lined up.' It always amazed Scott that Emily was so unimpressed that her father had been lead guitarist in the supergroup, Panic Mode. To Emily, Seth Wild was just your average nice-but-mildly-embarrassing dad. But to Scott, who played guitar in a band, and loved all kinds of retro music, Seth Wild was as much a hero as Jimi Hendrix or Eric Clapton, even though he'd retired from the music business years ago. 'He's even got Splinter Planet coming!'

'Who are Splinter Planet when they're at home?' Jack asked, reaching into his backpack for his personal chocolate supplies.

'*Who are Splinter Planet?*' Scott spluttered. 'That's like asking who are the Beatles? They started out in the 1970s and had about a million number ones before they split up. This'll be their first live performance since they re-formed last year.'

Jack shrugged. 'The 1970s? That's *prehistoric*.'

Emily laughed. 'Yeah, that megalosaurus fossil we found in the quarry at Christmas was probably at all their gigs.'

Scott aimed a grape at the back of Emily's head. 'Ha ha! I know they're ancient but their stuff is classic. And you must have heard of their guitarist? Nick Dylan's a total *legend*!'

'Of course I've heard of Nick Dylan,' Emily said.

'See,' Scott told Jack. 'At least *Emily* knows something about rock history!'

Emily grinned. 'Actually I've only heard of him because he checked into The Lighthouse this morning.'

Scott's jaw dropped open. 'You're kidding. *Nick Dylan* is staying at The Lighthouse? *The* Nick Dylan?'

'Yeah. And the rest of Splinter Planet as well. Dad's friends with them all.'

'That. Is. So. Cool!' Scott breathed.

But Emily had suddenly remembered something much more interesting than guitar heroes. She jumped up and pulled Scott to his feet. 'Wait till you see this! Stand there and stretch your arm out. You need to hold something in your hand.'

Jack fished in the picnic bag and held out a forgotten banana.

Emily nodded. 'Just the thing!'

Jack watched, enthralled. Scott looked a prize wally standing there, arm out, clutching a banana, as if feeding an invisible chimpanzee. It was such a pity there was no one else around to witness the sight. Then Jack had a brainwave. He sneaked his new phone out of his backpack under cover of a huge bar of white chocolate.

Emily stepped back three paces. She took a deep breath and squared her shoulders. All of a sudden she was leaping and spinning, her leg whizzing through the air in a blur of speed.

Her foot made contact with the banana.

The banana flew out of Scott's hand.

Jack stared at Emily, who was calmly brushing sand from her t-shirt. Then he looked down at his phone. *Oh, yes!* He'd caught it all. This photo was priceless! He'd save it up for a moment when he needed some heavy-duty ammunition! 'Wow! Where did you learn that, Em? It was like something out of *The Matrix*!'

Emily grinned. 'I've been doing kick-boxing lessons. After that horrible security guard chased us during Operation Dinosaur I figured I needed to learn self-defence.'

'Yes, well, good idea,' Scott mumbled, trying to claw back some shreds of dignity. 'Of course, I could've blocked you if I'd known you were going to do a roundhouse kick.'

Jack laughed. 'That's the element of surprise! You don't give your enemies a five-minute warning.'

Scott swore to himself he would *never* let anything this uncool happen again. He would sign up for a crash course in martial arts the instant he got back to London.

Emily turned to Jack. 'You want to have a go?'

Jack lay back on the rock. Emily was scary enough as it was, even without a black belt in kick-boxing. 'Nah, you're OK. I never spar on a full stomach.' It was true, he *had* scarfed down rather more of that white chocolate than was strictly advisable in a single sitting.

Drift dropped the mangled banana at Scott's feet, eagerly waiting for him to launch it into orbit again. But suddenly the little dog pricked up his ears – first the black one, then the white one with brown spots. He dashed to the water's edge and barked at the waves.

The three friends sprinted into the shallows after him. When Drift's ears went into Listening Formation like this, he was never mistaken. And yet, there was not a sound to be heard above the constant crashing of the waves and the wailing of the seagulls.

Emily ran back to *Gemini* and grabbed her binoculars. She swept the expanse of water between the cliffs: nothing but dark patches of seaweed and gulls bobbing on the waves.

'What's that?' Jack cried, pointing towards the rocks where the cove narrowed. Scott shaded his eyes with his hand. 'It could be a seal . . .'

Suddenly Emily spotted the shape moving in the water.

She knew what a seal looked like.

It wasn't a seal.

Two

Not Bad!

Scott took the binoculars and adjusted the focus.

Now he saw it, too. An arm shot up and then sank beneath a wave. A face appeared for a moment, the mouth open in a scream. Then it was gone.

There was a man in the water.

The three friends stared at the spot in silence. The man couldn't have swum out from shore. They'd had the tiny beach to themselves all morning and there was nowhere else in the cove where you could climb down from the cliffs – unless you were a mountain goat with full abseiling gear. He must have jumped – or fallen – from a boat. And yet there were no boats to be seen.

'What's he doing?' Jack murmured, taking his turn with the binoculars.

'*Drowning*, by the look of it,' Scott replied. Suddenly, as if the words had snapped them out of a hypnotic trance, they all raced up the beach towards *Gemini*. They tugged the little boat across the sand and into the water. Drift jumped aboard, then Emily and Jack. Scott gave the final push before leaping in, like the last man of a bobsleigh team. Jack had already pulled on his life jacket and snatched up the oars. He rowed as hard as he could until his face blazed crimson. Scott took over before he exploded.

Emily knelt in the bow and called out directions. Her heart was hammering so hard she could barely hold the binoculars steady. On the way to the beach, she'd navigated a safe course well away from the treacherous rocks – there was a clear channel to the east side of the cove if you knew where to find it. But the drowning man had been washed deep into the minefield of jagged crags and barely submerged reefs. Here the waves tumbled over each other, barging and shoving through the rocks like a rioting crowd, in their rush to reach the shore.

'Let me take the oars,' she shouted to Scott. 'I know these rocks better than you do.'

Emily steered *Gemini* through the labyrinth. Scott and Jack clung to the sides and Drift cowered under the bench-seat as the little boat bucked and pitched in the churning foam.

Suddenly there was a stomach-turning crunch.

Scott checked the bow of the boat for damage. 'We're OK! It's not gone through the hull!'

'We can't risk going any further into the rocks,' Emily yelled over the crash of the waves. 'We'll be smashed to pieces.'

Jack grabbed a coil of rope. 'Let's throw him a line.'

Emily shook her head. 'It won't reach!' Then she whipped round as she heard a splash behind her.

Scott had dived over the side.

As he hit the water, the cold shocked the breath out of Scott's lungs. He'd thought the shallows near the beach were chilly, but this was a whole new dimension of cold. Above the surface the April sunshine felt like summer. In the sea, it was still mid-winter. Scott felt as if blades of ice were flaying the skin from his bones.

He kicked down hard to brace himself against the current and looked around for the drowning man. Spotting a shadow in the trough between two waves, he struck out towards it.

Scott was a strong swimmer but this was a world

away from notching up lengths in the pool. Every time he thought he was getting somewhere another mountain of salt water crashed over his head, scouring his throat and nostrils and stinging his eyes. The rocks scraped his feet and knees and elbows.

At last he emerged spluttering from beneath a breaker and found the man only a few metres away in the froth of white water. But the split second of triumph was immediately washed away. The man was floating with his head down. *Too late!* Disappointment sapped Scott's energy, but he forced himself to keep treading water. He rolled the body onto its back and wrapped his arm round its chest to drag it back to the boat. But suddenly the body twisted and the arms began to thrash. The man was alive! But he was panicking! He clung to Scott's shoulders. Scott choked as a wave caught him full in the face, and only his life jacket stopped the sea from sucking him under. The man clutched at him again.

I think I liked this guy better when he was dead, Scott thought, prising a tentacle-like arm from his neck. This was like wrestling with a giant octopus.

'Stop struggling,' Scott yelled at the top of his voice, 'or we'll both drown!'

It seemed to do the trick. The man relaxed and let Scott tow him in a floundering semi-backstroke towards the boat. 'What's your name?' Scott panted. But the man only mumbled a few meaningless words. Then he passed out.

At last Scott heard a rope slap into the water behind him. He caught hold of the end and Jack and Emily reeled him in. Between them they bundled the drowning man over the side. Scott clambered in after him.

Emily threw a towel around Scott, then began to weave her way out of the rocks and row for shore. Jack knelt on the floor of the boat and examined the man. He looked terrible. In fact, he looked worse than terrible. He looked *dead*. His face was grey, his lips were blue and a ragged gash split his forehead. More importantly, he wasn't breathing.

'He needs CPR!' Scott's voice was muffled by the towel over his head. 'You know how to do it.'

It was true. Jack had done a life-saving course at his BMX club – all the riders had to in case someone came off their bike. Now he wished he'd spent more time listening and less time laughing at his mate, Ali, doing a ventriloquist act with his plastic dummy. He remembered the basics: chest compressions and rescue breaths. But how many? In what order? *Just do it!* Jack told himself. *The guy's not going to be counting!* He gulped down some air, pinched the man's nose and blew into his mouth. Then he crossed his hands on the base of the rib cage and began to pump.

'I've called the coastguard,' Emily said. 'The lifeboat should get here any minute.'

'You got a signal on your mobile in these cliffs?' Scott asked through chattering teeth.

Emily shook her head and pointed to the waterproof bag under the seat. 'VHF radio. Dad got it for when I'm out in *Gemini* – ever since that little incident when Simon Fox tried to maroon us on Gulliver's Island last summer.'

Suddenly Jack stopped the compressions and sprang back. The man made a gurgling sound and water began gushing out of his mouth. It didn't spout in a fountain like in the cartoons. It was more of a retch-and-dribble effect. But it seemed to help. The man sighed and opened his eyes for a moment. Then he flopped back again. But this time he was breathing.

Emily cheered. 'Well done, Jack. You did it! That was brilliant!'

'Yeah,' Scott said from under his towel. 'Not bad!'

'And Scott as well, of course,' Emily added. 'The way you jumped in and rescued him was amazing!'

Jack gave Scott a thumbs-up. 'Yeah. Not bad!'

The boys exchanged grins. They didn't make a habit of heaping praise on each other. They both considered the other's head quite big enough already without any further encouragement, but they were prepared to make an exception in this case. *Not bad* was as good as it got!

At last they reached the beach and laid the mystery man out in the recovery position on the warm sand. They were covering him with towels and blankets when suddenly Drift started his barking-at-the-water routine again.

Please not someone else drowning! Jack thought. *I don't think I can go through that again!* But then he heard the buzz of an outboard motor.

The lifeboat was approaching.

Three

Observation and Deduction

Within minutes, the two coastguards had thanked the friends for their brave actions, swaddled the man in foil survival blankets and transferred him onto the lifeboat for the trip back to Castle Key harbour. From there he'd be sped by ambulance to Carrickstowe Hospital on the mainland. They'd insisted Scott go with them for a check-up too; he had several nasty scrapes and bruises from the razor-sharp rocks.

Jack, Emily and Drift were left behind on the tiny beach. When they'd finished stowing the picnic things aboard *Gemini* for the trip home, Emily flopped down on the sand and stared out across the cove. Drift curled up beside her for a snooze.

Jack sank down next to them. 'Ah, yes!' he sighed contentedly. 'The Mystery of the Drowning Man. It's a shame you'll be too busy cooking and cleaning to investigate, Em,' he teased. 'Scott and I will just have to solve it by ourselves . . .'

Emily snorted. 'You two promised to help me at The Lighthouse, remember? And anyway, you wouldn't get *anywhere* without me!'

'Oh, yes, we would!' Jack chanted the words as if he were playing the part of an ugly sister in a pantomime.

Emily laughed. 'OK. If you're so sure, tell me – who exactly is our mystery man and how did he end up in the water?'

Jack laughed. 'Funnily enough, we didn't get round to swapping our life stories while I was blowing air into his lungs.'

Emily sighed. 'I meant using your powers of observation and deduction.'

Jack groaned to himself. He had a horrible feeling Emily was going to beat him hands down at this game. He stood up, selected a flat pebble from the beach and skimmed it across the shallow water. 'Oh, yeah! Six bounces! Beat that!'

Emily gave him a look that told him there was no point trying to sidetrack her with a sneaky change of subject.

'OK,' Jack said. 'I *observed* that he was a big guy. Dead heavy to pull onto the boat. And his chest was a lot more solid than a plastic dummy's.'

'Is that all?'

Jack shrugged.

Emily picked up a stone and sent it soaring over the water. Only three bounces. She frowned. 'Our mystery man is about sixty years old. He lives in a warm country and he works outside, probably doing heavy manual labour. He usually wears a hat. He's married to a woman called Rosa. He's a heavy smoker and he was involved in a nasty accident some time ago.'

Jack gaped at Emily. She had to be bluffing. There was no way you could tell all that from a half-drowned body. 'Yeah, right,' he said, trying to sound unimpressed. 'And I suppose he has a cat called Mr Tibbles, likes a game of Scrabble and is allergic to gherkins . . .'

Emily took her time selecting another pebble and took aim again. Only two bounces this time.

'Go on, then, tell me how you figured it all out!' Jack sighed. 'I know you're going to anyway.'

Emily smiled in a manner that Jack could only describe as slightly smug. 'He's got grey hair and more wrinkles than my dad, but he's not completely ancient, so I'm saying about sixty. He's white but he's got a tan, which means he must work outside. Probably somewhere hotter than here or he wouldn't be so brown this early in the year.'

'Aha!' Jack cried. 'What if he's just been to Spain on holiday? Maybe he's been sitting by the pool for the last two weeks.'

Emily shook her head. 'He's got t-shirt tan-lines. You don't sunbathe in your t-shirt. He had a tan line across his forehead too, which is how I know he usually wears a hat.'

'I can see how you get the manual work,' Jack conceded. 'He was pretty muscly. But what about the smoking?'

'Yellow nicotine stains on his fingers.'

'And the accident in the past?'

'Scars on his arms. Not just the bumps and bruises from today but old ones, too.'

Jack shook his head. 'OK, but I'm still not buying that you know his wife's name.'

Emily launched another stone. Still only two bounces. 'Wedding ring,' she said. 'And a small tattoo on his left arm.' She handed Jack her mobile phone. 'I took a photo of it before the coastguard arrived.'

'Of course you did,' Jack muttered, shading the screen from the sun. The photo showed a tattoo of the word *Rosa* surrounded by hearts and flowers. 'Doesn't mean she's his wife.'

'He'd have had it removed if she was an old girlfriend,'

Emily said confidently, as if she were suddenly an international expert on tattoo culture. *Honestly,* Jack thought, *sometimes Emily can be* almost *as annoying as Scott.*

Suddenly Jack spotted the perfect stone: smooth, round and flat as a Rich Tea biscuit. He fired it across the water . . . seven, eight, nine bounces! That had to be a world record!

At least he could beat Emily at *something.* 'Did you see that?' he crowed.

'Sorry. What?' Emily glanced up from studying the tattoo on her phone. 'We'd better get going. It's a long row back without Scott to help us.'

'Grrr!' Jack fumed, as they pushed *Gemini* into the water. Emily hadn't even *seen* his mighty nine-bouncer! 'Drift, did *you* see it?'

Drift licked Jack's knee, hoping that was the right answer.

Jack groaned. 'You were fast asleep, weren't you, Drifty? Yet again, my genius goes unnoticed!' He took the oars and rowed for a while in silence, the entire rescue operation running in his head like a film. Suddenly he remembered something about the drowning man. Something highly observational *and* deductive! 'He was wearing a t-shirt, jeans and brown boots. I guess that tells us he wasn't exactly planning to go in for a dip.'

Emily grinned. 'Right! So, did he fall or was he pushed?'

Jack looked up at the cliffs that surrounded Keyhole Cove. The afternoon sun had melted to an orange fireball and was sinking towards the western rim, throwing the sheer rock-face into shadow. The cliffs were nowhere near as high as the ones below the castle in Key Bay, but they were still pretty imposing. 'Could he even have survived if he fell from there?'

Emily frowned. 'I don't know. He *did* have a lot of injuries.'

'So did Scott,' Jack pointed out. 'The two of them were being hurled around in those waves like socks in a washing machine.'

'Ooh, remember that big gash on his forehead? I bet he was hit over the head and dumped overboard from a passing boat.' Suddenly Emily's dark eyes were sparkling with excitement.

'But why?' Jack asked.

'Could be a million reasons.' Emily counted them off on her fingers. 'He was part of a drug smuggling operation that went wrong, or he was a spy who knew too much and had to be *eradicated*, or . . .'

Jack laughed. He'd wondered how long it would be before Emily linked their mystery man to the world of espionage or international drug smuggling. Or, preferably, both!

They'd left Keyhole Cove behind and were now rowing past the next inlet along the coast, where Pencarrick Point – a narrow spur of land ending in a huge flat-topped boulder thirty feet high – jutted out into the sea. Thrill-seekers flocked from miles away to jump from the top and do the famous 'Pencarrick Plummet'. On the way to Keyhole Cove that morning the friends had taken a break from rowing and watched for a while as a group of Russian tourists threw themselves off the rock like lemmings.

Jack had wanted to give it a try but Emily had talked him out of it. If you misjudged the angle of your jump, she'd warned, you could be hurt on the rocks below. Secretly Jack had been slightly relieved. The leaping, plummeting and splash-landing part looked awesome, but he wasn't the strongest swimmer in the world, and it looked like a long way back to the beach.

There were still people up on Pencarrick Point now. Their screams and laughter carried across the water. There was a resounding splash as a large woman in a wetsuit bombed into the water.

All at once, Jack had a flash of inspiration. 'Of course! Mystery Man was doing the Pencarrick Plummet, but he got it wrong. He hit his head on a rock and was washed into Keyhole Cove by the current.' He dropped the oars and blew smoke from the gun barrels he made with his fingers. He grinned at Emily, challenging her to deny the sharp-shooting brilliance of his logic.

'He jumped in fully-clothed with his boots on?' Emily asked.

Jack sighed. Trust Emily to pick on the one

miniscule loophole in his theory! But he wasn't going to be thwarted that easily. 'OK, then. He was up there watching and he *fell* in. Come on, admit it – it's far more likely than a passing boatload of spying smugglers. Or smuggling spies, even.'

'It might be more likely,' Emily said. 'But it's definitely not what happened.'

Four

The Pencarrick Plummet

Jack realized they were now bobbing around in circles and took up the oars again. 'How can you be so certain Mystery Man didn't fall in from Pencarrick Point?'

Emily tapped the side of her nose mysteriously. 'You should listen to Old Bob more often.'

Jack *had* listened to Old Bob – a fisherman who'd lived on Castle Key island since the beginning of time – but as he was usually reciting nuggets of ancient wisdom like *When seagulls fly high, there'll be eels in your pie* and *Never pick radishes on a Thursday*, Jack wasn't sure how it was going to help in the current situation.

'Old Bob's taught me loads of stuff about the tides and currents,' Emily explained. 'If you fell in from Pencarrick Point you wouldn't end up in Keyhole Cove. There's a strong rip-tide that would drag you out to sea and then you'd be washed back in somewhere further east. You'd probably end up somewhere below the Trago Gallery.' She pointed towards the headland up ahead. The art gallery with its Disneyland towers and spires sat perched on top of the cliffs like a princess's crown from a dressing-up box.

Jack wasn't convinced. 'I still think we should go and check it out. Someone up on the rock might have seen something suspicious.'

Emily thought for a moment. Although she was sure the man hadn't jumped or fallen from Pencarrick Point, Jack was right: you could see for miles from up on that rock. Someone could have spotted a cargo ship hijacked by smugglers or a speedboat driven by a ruthless secret agent. 'OK. But we'll need to go in undercover. If I'm right, we could be dealing with some very dangerous elements. We don't want them finding out we've been asking too many questions.'

A few moments later Jack and Emily had moored *Gemini* to a small wooden jetty and were scrambling up the winding path onto the rocky point. Drift scampered ahead, delighted that they had stopped for another walk.

'We pretend we want to do the plummet,' Jack suggested as they climbed. He wasn't really buying Emily's Dangerous Element theory, but he was happy to play along. 'And we act all nervous so we can ask loads of questions about whether anyone has ever got injured or anything.'

'On one condition,' Emily agreed. 'No jumping in! I'm definitely not coming in to rescue you. And I'm double definitely not giving you the kiss of life!'

At the top Emily did a quick survey. Several groups of young people were lounging around on the flat expanse of rock, enjoying the late afternoon sunshine. Music played from portable speakers, and picnic leftovers were strewn across rugs and blankets. Drift pounced joyfully on an abandoned sausage roll, scattering the rival gangs of seagulls that had been scrapping over it. Every now and then there were countdowns, and screams could be heard as someone ventured to the edge of the rock and jumped off.

Sidling close to the nearest group, Emily struck up a loud debate with Jack. 'We need to check out whether it's safe first,' she said. 'It looks dangerous.'

'I'll jump if you will,' Jack replied.

One of the group, a skinny young man in surfer shorts and a college-football shirt, looked up from playing a game on his phone. 'Hey, just go for it, guys! Why not hold hands and jump together? Romantic, eh?'

The girl next to him batted him on the head with her magazine. 'Don't encourage the boy!' She laughed. 'You can see his poor girlfriend is terrified.'

Emily was so taken aback she almost burst out laughing and blew their cover. Being thought of as a) Jack's girlfriend, or b) terrified, was almost worse than falling into the hands of enemy agents. But she pulled herself together. She would do it for the sake of the investigation! 'So, you've never seen anyone get hurt?' she asked, clinging to Jack's arm and sounding as nervous as she could.

'Nothing to it!' the skinny man laughed. 'As long as you jump well away from the cliff face.'

'Have you ever seen anyone hit the rocks and get washed out to sea?' Jack asked.

'What about boats?' Emily asked. 'Have there been any unusual vessels near here today? It could be dangerous if you, er, swam into one,' she added, a little lamely.

The girl laughed and stared at Emily and Jack over her enormous sunglasses. 'You two have got over-active imaginations! Nobody's hit the rocks. Nobody's been eaten by sharks. Nobody's been mowed down by a passing ship!'

Jack and Emily hung around and chatted some more. They soon learned that most of the people on the rock were camping at Roshendra Farm or staying in the youth hostel in Tregower.

'We're all here for the music festival,' the girl with the sunglasses explained. 'I'm a big Splinter Planet fan. I'm really into that whole eighties scene. Nick Dylan's my all-time hero. I can't wait to see him.'

Emily decided not to mention that she'd seen the 'all-time hero' having his breakfast in The Lighthouse dining room that very morning. He'd been wearing a hairnet over his trademark mane of golden hair, and was complaining that the milk on his cereal was too cold for his sensitive teeth. Hero hadn't exactly been the first word that sprang to mind as she'd warmed a second bowl of Coco Pops in the microwave for him.

However, nobody had seen anything remotely suspicious. Specifically, there were no reported sightings of a sixty-year-old man falling off Pencarrick Point, or of a boatload of spies or smugglers.

Jack and Emily wandered towards the edge of the rock and looked down at the waves below.

'It doesn't look that far,' Jack commented. He watched a short, stocky man fling himself into the sea, legs and arms flailing. In fact, the Pencarrick Plummet looked really awesome. Yes, he was definitely going to do it! He'd worry about swimming back to the beach later.

He was pulling off his t-shirt when Emily suddenly grabbed his arm. 'Feeling dizzy,' she groaned, staggering backwards and stumbling against a small plastic barrel someone had been using as a makeshift seat. The barrel went flying over the precipice, plummeting into the waves.

'What's the matter?' Jack asked, pulling Emily away from the edge, with help from Drift who placed himself courageously between Emily and the drop in case she had another funny turn. 'You're not afraid of heights! Were you *that* desperate to stop me jumping?'

'Shh!' Emily whispered. 'I just wanted to make it look like an accident.'

'What?'

'Knocking that barrel over the edge.'

'Why?'

'It's an experiment!'

'How?' Jack wished Emily would stop talking in riddles!

Emily sighed. 'To prove that if Mystery Man went into the water here he wouldn't be washed towards Keyhole Cove, of course.'

They stood and watched as the plastic barrel was sucked under the waves. Then it popped back up and bobbed along. A seagull landed on it, then fell off as the barrel shot out from under its feet. It looked around as if to check nobody had noticed. Jack laughed. He'd never seen a seagull look embarrassed before.

Just as Emily had predicted, the barrel floated out

to sea and drifted east towards the headland – in the opposite direction from Keyhole Cove.

'We'll fish it out of the water on our way home,' Emily said.

Jack nodded and grinned. Then he looked nervously over his shoulder. Emily had been right about so many things today he was *almost* starting to believe she might be right about secret agents lurking in the crowd, intent on sending anyone who asked too many questions about the drowning man to a watery grave.

Five

It Wasn't Chris!

Meanwhile, Scott was being treated for an assortment of minor injuries in the Accident and Emergency department of Carrickstowe Hospital. A nurse called Penny Miller – a large, round lady with curly white hair and bearing a close resemblance to Mother Christmas – had applied industrial quantities of antiseptic cream to his cuts and grazes. It stung like crazy – as if he'd been rolling naked in an ant-infested nettle patch (not that Scott had ever *tried* rolling naked in an ant-infested nettle patch, of course).

But apart from the ant-and-nettle experience, he was rather enjoying himself. The doctors and nurses were all treating him like a war hero, bringing him hot drinks and chocolate bars and congratulating him on saving the drowning man's life. They also brought him a mirror so he could admire the V-shaped cut that sliced across his cheekbone, the edges now neatly stuck together with little pieces of tape. Scott thought it gave him the dangerously dashing look of a swashbuckling pirate. 'Tis but a flesh wound,' he muttered to his reflection. It was going to be the kind of scar you could tell stories about for years to come. *Ah, yes, that's from the time I single-handedly rescued a man from a storm-tossed sea.* He wondered whether he could get away with throwing in a shark attack for good measure . . .

The drowning man had been rushed off to a ward on the other side of the hospital. He hadn't regained consciousness on the journey from Keyhole Cove, except when he sat bolt upright in the ambulance, declared, 'It wasn't Chris,' and then passed out again.

It wasn't Chris. Scott turned the words over in his mind as he perched on the bed in his cubicle waiting for Nurse Miller to come and give him the all-clear to go home. *It wasn't Chris?* The paramedics had assumed the man was just rambling, but Scott knew instantly that those three words had to be important. Why? *Because he'd heard them before!* The man had mumbled exactly the same thing when they were floundering around in the sea together.

It wasn't Chris.

But who was Chris and what didn't he do?

Scott's thoughts were interrupted by a white-coated doctor poking his head through the curtains. Dr Obi's yellow-tinged eyes were pouched with tiredness and at least two days' stubble covered his jaw, but he greeted Scott with a friendly smile and a warm handshake. 'Just came down from the ward to let you know that the man you rescued is doing well. He's got cuts and bruises and some broken ribs, but it's the bump on the head we're most concerned about. We won't know the effects of that until he comes round.'

'Do you know who he is yet?' Scott asked.

Dr Obi rubbed his temples. 'No. He had no ID on him. We'll have to wait until he regains consciousness. When he does, I'm sure he'll want to thank you in person. A few more minutes in the water and he wouldn't have made it.'

~

That evening Scott and Jack walked from Stone Cottage, where they were staying with their Great-aunt Kate, through the familiar narrow lanes of the old fishing village of Castle Key, and along the promontory to

The Lighthouse. They found Emily at the table in the first-floor kitchen, hulling strawberries and stoning cherries.

'Pull up a knife and join the party,' she said, rolling her eyes. 'The band's ordered fresh fruit smoothies with breakfast tomorrow.'

While they worked, Scott updated Jack and Emily on his trip to the hospital, ending with the mysterious words, 'It wasn't Chris.'

Emily fetched her notebook from her bedroom on the eighth floor. She'd already written *OPERATION DROWNING MAN* at the top of a new page and underlined it twice. She'd also added a numbered list of all the details about the man she'd figured out earlier, and a sketch of the Rosa tattoo. Now she wrote *It wasn't Chris* and circled the phrase in red. She stared down at the page as she skilfully slid a stone from a cherry with the tip of her knife. 'It wasn't Chris. I'm sure this is the key to the entire investigation,' she said. 'Could Chris be his contact in the spy ring? Or even the spymaster himself?'

Scott flinched as cherry juice flicked off Jack's knife and squirted him in the eye. 'I'm not sure about the spy angle. *I* think Mystery Man is trying to tell us that it wasn't Chris who threw him in the water.'

'Brilliant,' Jack said. 'That narrows it down no end. We can cross everyone in the world whose name is Chris off our suspect list. That only leaves about seven billion people.' He popped a mutilated strawberry into his mouth. 'In fact, we don't even know it's a man. Chris could be short for Christine, not Christopher.'

Emily grinned. 'And we know where he – or she – *didn't* go into the water as well. Our barrel experiment proved that it wasn't Pencarrick Point.' She slapped Jack's hand. 'You're not meant to be *eating* the strawberries!'

'So that leaves only five and a half trillion other possible locations on the planet,' Jack laughed, making up a number off the top of his head. 'Yep, if we keep going at this rate we should have this case cracked in, ooh, another three millennia!'

The friends continued to debate the possible ways that Mystery Man could have ended up in the sea as they worked their way through the fruit mountain: a parachute jump gone wrong (where was the parachute?), attempted suicide (where was the note?), or a bid to swim the English Channel by someone with a very poor sense of direction (in his boots?). Emily carefully listed the options in her notebook – even though she was still convinced the man was a spy.

'*What* is going on in here?' The scream came from Emily's mum. Maria Wild was standing in the doorway, hands clutching at her wild black hair, gasping as if her kitchen had been invaded by zombie werewolves. 'It looks like mass murder!'

Emily looked round and saw what she meant. The

walls and floor were spattered with red juice, their hands were stained a grisly scarlet and three knives lay dripping on the table. It was like a scene from a late-night horror film.

The friends were still cleaning up the carnage when they heard the front door open downstairs. 'That'll be Dad back with the band. They've been rehearsing up at the castle,' Emily said.

'Do you think we could go and talk to them?' Scott asked, suddenly feeling nervous.

Emily shrugged. 'If we must.'

Jack threw down his scrubbing brush. 'Anything's better than this!'

The members of Splinter Planet were sprawling on the sofas in the huge circular guest lounge. Billy Riordan, the bass player – a man with the powerful build of a heavyweight boxer, long jet-black hair and a craggy, hawk-like face – was recounting a stormy argument with their manager. His tale was peppered with so many swear words that if they'd all been beeped out, he'd have sounded like a smoke alarm going off.

Nick Dylan nodded vaguely while making adjustments to the gold, star-shaped electric guitar across his knees. His trademark, Goldilocks-style blond ringlets fell across his face so that, when he looked up, his wrinkles came as a surprise.

The drummer, meanwhile, was reading a copy of *Mathematics Today* and listening to music on his iPod, his fingers tapping out rhythms on the arm of his chair. If you looked up the word *cool* in a dictionary, Scott thought, you'd probably just find a picture of Flak Petersen, sporting a long, black leather coat, white crocodile-skin shoes and designer shades. His skin was so black it was almost blue, while his hair, cropped to the skull, was silver-white.

Everyone looked up as the door flew open. A pretty woman with short, flame-red hair, dressed in black leggings and a floaty top, staggered in beneath a mountain of carrier bags. Delicious aromas of coriander and cumin wafted into the room.

'That's Lauren Wade,' Emily whispered. 'Nick Dylan's girlfriend.'

Scott recognized Lauren as an actress he'd seen in a couple of episodes of a soap opera, playing the part of a hairdresser with a gambling problem.

'I picked up a takeaway in Carrickstowe,' Lauren announced, marching through to the dining room and setting foil trays out on a long table.

The band members fell on the food like a pack of ravenous hyenas.

'Tuck in if you want,' Nick Dylan called to Jack, Scott and Emily, who were still hovering near the spiral staircase. 'There's enough here to feed an army.'

Jack didn't need asking twice. That chicken tikka masala was calling his name.

Lauren spooned rice and curry onto a plate for Nick. 'I asked them to take the chillies out so it's not too spicy for you.'

'No chillies!' Jack whispered to Emily. 'That's not very rock 'n' roll, is it?'

But Scott ignored them. He was sharing a prawn korma with guitar god, Nick Dylan, for goodness' sake!

'So, Seth tells me you're a guitarist yourself, mate,' Nick said, reaching for the naan bread. 'What axe d'you use?'

'A Gibson SG.' Scott tried to sound casual. 'Customized it myself.'

'Sweet! Although I like the old Fender Stratocaster myself,' Nick said through a mouthful of korma. 'Come for a jam session with us one day.'

'As long as you don't overdo it!' Lauren warned. She turned to Scott. 'Nick needs his rest.'

Scott grinned so much he felt the tapes holding the cut on his cheek together stretch. This had to be in his top ten Best Days Ever. He'd pulled off a heroic rescue, sustained a wound that made him look like a pirate and *now* he was hanging out with Nick Dylan! A hat trick!

Jack thought it had been a pretty good day too: picnic on the beach, plenty of chocolate, strawberries and now a really good curry. All the major food groups!

And as for Emily? She had an unknown mystery man to identify. Two, in fact, if you counted Chris! What could be better?

Six

Identity Unknown

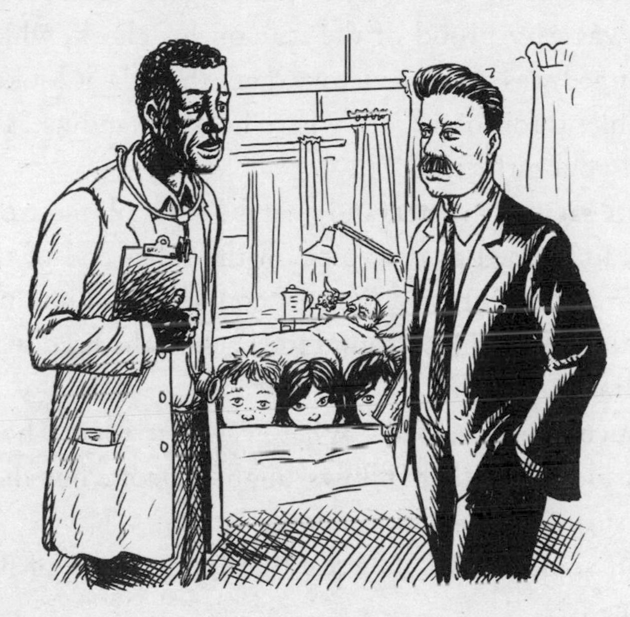

The following morning Jack woke to the sound of Scott's mobile phone belting out the Black Eyed Peas on the other side of the attic room they shared at Stone Cottage. Scott kept on snoring. Nothing short of a hand grenade would get him out of bed this early. Jack padded across the room and picked up the phone.

'Hello,' came a woman's voice. 'This is Nurse Penny Miller. Is that Scott?'

Jack slapped his hand over his mouth to stifle a snigger. Scott had been handing out his phone number to nurses at the hospital! Doing his Teenage Superhero act again, no doubt! Who did he think he was? Justin Bieber?

'Oy, Scarface!' Jack yelled, jumping on Scott's bed. Scott was very proud of the scar on his cheek, which he claimed was a V for victory. Jack thought it looked more like L for loser from where he was standing. 'It's one of your girlfriends!'

Scott sat up, yawned and snatched the phone from Jack. He listened to the voice on the other end of the line for a moment, said 'Yes, of course,' and hung up. Then he walloped Jack round the back of the head with his pillow.

'Youch!' Jack yelped. 'What was that for?' Those old-fashioned feather pillows might be soft, but they made surprisingly solid weapons.

Scott sighed. 'FYI, Nurse Miller is not "one of my girlfriends"!'

'What did you give her your number for, then?'

'She was phoning to say that Mystery Man has come round and he's asking to meet his rescuer . . .'

'Well, I guess I could squeeze a visit into my busy schedule.' Jack ducked as the pillow swung towards his head again.

Scott tried to burrow back under his blankets. 'He meant me, not you!'

Jack pulled the blankets away. 'Hel-lo! Who gave him the kiss of life? And what about Emily's epic rowing skills getting us through the rocks? And we wouldn't even have seen him if Drift hadn't raised the alarm.'

Scott held up his hands. 'OK, keep your hair on. It was a team effort. We'll all go. I can't wait to find out who he is.'

'Nor me,' Jack was already searching under his bed for a pair of socks. But suddenly he hesitated. 'What if Em's right and this guy's a spy, but he's some kind of evil *enemy* spy and he tries to kill us so we don't find out what he's up to?'

Scott rolled his eyes. 'You've definitely been spending too much time with Emily!'

~

Meanwhile Emily was helping to serve breakfast at The Lighthouse. Sunshine poured in through the big glass windows of the dining room, which was housed in a conservatory on the side of the original red-and-white striped tower. It was still early and only one guest was up. Flak Petersen had been out for a run and was now sipping an espresso and reading the morning papers.

Emily hummed happily to herself as she set the smoothies out on the tables. Although Mum had been furious about the 'berry bloodbath' last night, it had finally made her realize she needed to take on some extra help during the festival. Vicky White from Roshendra Farm had agreed to come in for a few hours each day, which meant that as soon as she'd finished the breakfast shift, Emily would have plenty of time to work on Operation Drowning Man. She laughed out loud. The boys had promised to help with her chores so she got more free time. Their 'help' had worked better than she could ever have expected!

Flak glanced over the top of the *Financial Times*. Emily swiftly disguised her laugh as a polite cough, but the cough turned into a snort of surprise as she caught sight of *The Carrickstowe Times*, lying on the table. Grabbing the paper, she hurried out of the dining room into the empty guest lounge, sank down on a sofa and stared at the front page headline: LOCAL KIDS RESCUE MAN FROM KEYHOLE COVE – IDENTITY UNKNOWN!

'Oh, no, this is terrible,' Emily breathed to Drift, who'd jumped up onto her lap. Drift cocked his head to one side and did his Question Mark ears – bent over at the top and pointing outwards.

'Whoever bashed this guy on the head and dumped him in the sea obviously wanted him dead,' Emily explained. 'If they see this story in the paper they'll realize that they messed up. They'll want to come back and finish the job. Mystery Man could be in serious danger.'

Drift raised his spotted ear. He had no idea what

Emily was talking about, but he was a very good listener.

'OK, I *know* that Mystery Man might have fallen in the water *accidentally*,' Emily told him. 'But we have to think Worst Case Scenario until we know otherwise! We'd better phone Scott and Jack and arrange a surveillance operation.'

Emily fell silent as she heard someone coming into the guest lounge. She couldn't help blushing. She talked to Drift all the time, but she knew not everyone thought that conducting in-depth conversations with a dog was exactly normal. Luckily, Lauren Wade – padding in wearing a long, silk dressing gown and fluffy slippers – didn't seem to notice.

'Do you have any herbal tea?' she asked. 'Nick is feeling a bit delicate this morning. I don't want him disturbed until at least midday.'

Emily started making a pot of peppermint tea. She'd nearly finished when Scott called to tell her that Mystery Man had regained consciousness.

She shoved the tea tray into Lauren's hands and made for the door. Like Scott and Jack, Emily couldn't wait to find out the truth about the unknown man they'd pulled from the sea.

~

The three friends met near the common and cycled across the island and over the narrow causeway to the hospital on the outskirts of Carrickstowe. The boys had brought their bikes with them on the train from London and Emily, as always, had her trusty bike with the special basket on the back for Drift. Unfortunately dogs weren't allowed in the hospital (Emily considered disguising Drift as a guide dog but the boys persuaded her it would never work), so Drift took up position in his basket and remained outside on Lookout Duty.

As they entered the ward, Emily noticed a familiar figure stop at the nurses' station. He straightened the creases in his immaculately pressed trousers, smoothed down his glistening black moustache and asked to speak to Dr Obi.

Detective Inspector Hassan! He had to be here to see the drowning man. Which meant she was right; Mystery Man *was* mixed up in spying or smuggling or some other shady underworld activities. Determined to find out more, Emily dived into the gap between two empty beds, pulling the boys with her.

They listened as D. I. Hassan questioned the doctor, whose white coat was buttoned askew over his crumpled shirt and tie. 'Has the patient been able to tell you what happened yet?'

'Not yet, I'm afraid,' Dr Obi replied. 'He has profound retrograde amnesia.'

D. I. Hassan rocked back on his heels and nodded wisely, as if he knew what the doctor was talking about.

'Severe loss of memory for the time before the head

injury,' Dr Obi explained. 'The memories usually come back gradually but there are no guarantees. Brain scans will give us more of an idea, but at the moment he doesn't even remember who he is, let alone how he came to be in the water.'

Memory loss? Huddled in the gap between the beds, Emily felt a twinge of disappointment; they weren't going to find out who the drowning man was. But the disappointment was immediately pushed aside by a jolt of excitement; the mystery of the drowning man had just got even *more* mysterious.

Meanwhile Jack made a mental note to remember the phrase *profound retrograde amnesia*. That could come in very handy next time Miss Taylor sprang a surprise history test on him.

'What about his injuries?' D. I. Hassan asked Dr Obi. 'Any sign that they could have been caused *before* he entered the water?'

'Cuts, bruises, three broken ribs. A nasty bump on the forehead. It's all consistent with impact with the rocks. Either falling from a height or just being hurled against them in the waves. There are some possible defence injuries on the hands, but he could have scraped his knuckles on the rocks.'

'Defence injuries!' Emily whispered to the boys. 'That proves he was fighting before he went in the water. I told you someone tried to kill him.'

'*Possible* defence injuries!" Scott whispered back.

D. I. Hassan sighed. 'Well, we've not found a suicide note or had any missing persons reports in yet. He probably just wandered off after a row with his wife and fell in.'

Emily tutted to herself. Why did the police always have to assume the most boring explanation for everything?

'We'll run his fingerprints through our database,' D. I. Hassan continued. 'If he's got a criminal record we'll find a match. But I'm sure someone'll turn up and claim him before then. In the meantime, call me if he starts to remember anything. We've asked hospital security to keep watch in case anyone comes looking for him. We can't rule out foul play at this stage.'

At last! Emily thought. *That's more like it! Although if it was up to me, I'd have a round-the-clock armed guard ready for when the killer comes back to finish the job.*

D. I. Hassan shook hands with Dr Obi and left.

'Excuse me! What are you three doing down there?'

'Um, er . . .' Jack looked up to see a stern-faced nurse, her dark hair scraped back into a tightly knotted bun, glowering down at them. He prided himself on being able to come up with the killer excuse for any tricky situation, but right now he couldn't think of a single reason why they were crawling around on the hospital floor. He was about to attempt something feeble to do with inspecting hospital cleaning standards when . . .

'They're looking for my remote control. I dropped it.'

Jack almost jumped out his skin. The quavering voice came from the empty bed behind him. Except now he saw that it *wasn't* empty; it was occupied by a frail old man who was lying so still he hardly wrinkled the crisp white sheet. 'Oh, no, here it is,' the man croaked. 'It was on the bed all the time.'

The nurse – Sandra Redpath, according to her name badge – planted her hands on her hips and swept the friends with a suspicious glare. 'I've got my eye on you three!' She turned and marched away.

Jack, Scott and Emily all whispered their thanks to the old man.

'Don't mention it!' he said, holding out his hand. 'Harry Stiles. Pleased to meet you!'

Jack grinned. If anyone tried to come back and silence Mystery Man, they'd have to get past Nurse Redpath and Harry Stiles first!

Seven

Good Old-fashioned Investigating

Mystery Man was on the other side of the six-bed ward. Despite the peach-coloured hospital gown and the bandage round his head, he looked a great deal better than the last time Jack had seen him. He didn't have water spewing out of his mouth for a start.

The friends introduced themselves and pulled up chairs around the bed.

'Hey, guys. So you're the ones who saved my life?

Let's just hope I turn out to be a millionaire and I can stump up a big fat reward!'

Jack laughed as if money was the furthest thing from his mind, although secretly he couldn't deny the thought had occurred to him too!

'Are you sure you can't remember *anything* about how you ended up in the water?' Emily asked, cutting to the chase as usual.

The man shrugged, wincing at the pain in his ribs. 'I don't remember a thing. I was hoping that seeing my rescuers would trigger something, but so far, no dice.'

'So you don't know who Rosa is?' Jack pointed to the tattoo.

'Does the name Chris ring any bells?' Scott asked.

The man just frowned. 'It's like someone just rubbed everything out.'

'How's our patient doing this morning?' Dr Obi strode to the bedside and made a note on his chart.

'Fine, I guess. Although I'd feel a whole lot better if I knew who I was. I could be a serial killer for all I know.' The man laughed, but his laughter had a nervous, slightly manic, edge to it. He kept chewing his lip and tapping his fingers on the sides of the bed. Not surprising really, Scott thought. There were one or two things he wouldn't mind forgetting himself – Emily kicking the banana out of his hand, for a start – but, on balance, losing your memory must be a terrifying experience.

'Well, you're clearly American from your accent,' Emily said. 'And we think that you're a builder or do some other kind of heavy work outdoors.'

Dr Obi rubbed his palms over his stubbly jaw and smiled down at the patient. 'These kids are quite the detectives! They're right. Arm and shoulder muscles over-developed, wear and tear on the spine, and our hearing tests reveal considerable hearing loss. Putting that together, my best guess is that you've been working on the roads operating a pneumatic drill or jackhammer. You have to wear ear protection now, of course, but in the old days nobody realized the noise was harmful . . .'

'Sorry, what was that?' the man asked, cupping his hand behind his ear.

'I said the noise was harmful!' Dr Obi shouted. Then he grinned, realizing the man was joking.

Jack laughed admiringly. This guy may have lost his memory but he hadn't lost his sense of humour!

Moments later, Nurse Redpath returned, insisting that Mystery Man needed to rest.

'Don't worry!' Emily told him, as they were shooed away from the bed. 'We'll find out who you are if it's the last thing we do!'

The friends adjourned to the café in the hospital concourse, where the smell of burned coffee and toasted sandwiches competed with the general hospital-y whiff of medicine and disinfectant.

Scott fetched Cokes and chocolate chip cookies. Emily took out her notebook, annoyed to see that her neat lists and charts were besmirched with splashes of cherry juice. She turned to a clean page and wrote *Who is the drowning man??????* She added six question marks. It was, after all, a *very* big question.

'Our main priority is protecting him,' she told the boys. 'D. I. Hassan may think this is something to do with a family argument, but I'm sure the killer – almost certainly some kind of hired assassin or secret agent – will return to finish the job.'

Jack took a glug of his Coke. 'But I thought we'd just decided this guy was a road worker, not a spy? Unless, of course, he was spying for a rival road company!'

'Yeah,' Scott said. 'He must be trying to discover the secret formula for a new kind of tarmac that would enable his evil masters to take over the entire road network!'

Emily nodded seriously. 'Ooh, yeah, that could be it.'

Jack laughed. 'We were joking!'

Emily kicked them both under the table.

Scott grinned. Then he felt a bit mean. Sometimes winding Emily up was just *too* easy. 'Em's right about one thing,' he said, trying to make up for the teasing. 'Being on a road gang *would* be a great disguise for an undercover stake-out. You could be digging up the road outside Buckingham Palace and nobody would think anything of it.'

Jack wasn't convinced, but Emily insisted they had to keep watch for anyone suspicious entering the hospital. And since they weren't allowed on the ward, the café was the only viable Observation Post. Scott volunteered to take first shift.

Meanwhile, Jack and Emily would do some good old-fashioned investigating. The plan was to make enquiries at Carrickstowe Marina and all the boat-hire companies on Castle Key island. After all, if Mystery Man had been pushed off a boat, Emily figured someone might remember hiring a boat out to two men, but only one of them returning.

'It's a bit of a long shot, isn't it?' Jack grumbled. 'We've got more chance of finding the Lost City of Atlantis!'

Emily snapped her notebook shut. 'Do you have any better ideas?'

Jack had to admit he didn't. And anything was better than sitting around in the hospital café. The cookies tasted of antiseptic!

~

Their first stop was the brand new marina beyond the old Carrickstowe docks, where every kind of vessel was available for hire – from thirty-foot yachts to traditional fishing boats to jet skis and pedalos. Jack and Emily traipsed up and down piers and jetties, asking people if they would mind 'answering a few questions for a school project on tourism trends in Cornwall'.

Jack conducted the interviews while Emily jotted down their answers in her notebook, which she'd attached to the clipboard she kept in her bag as part of her investigations kit; she'd discovered that people would tell you *anything* if you had a clipboard. Meanwhile, Drift had a lovely time stalking the seagulls that thronged the marina.

'So taking yesterday as an example,' Jack asked casually at each hire company, 'how many boats went out? How many people hired each boat? How many people *returned* each boat?' Nobody took much notice of the peculiar questions slipped into the middle of a long survey. They just rattled off their answers, impatient to get back to swabbing down decks or filling out paperwork.

Nobody mentioned a boat coming back minus one passenger.

Giving up on the marina, Jack and Emily pedalled back over the causeway and along the west coast of Castle Key, repeating the same routine at the small boat-hire companies in Tregower and on Westward Beach. Still they had no luck.

'I told you this was a hopeless idea,' Jack griped.

'There are four boatyards in Key Bay we haven't tried yet,' Emily snapped.

'Ooh, I can't wait!' Jack muttered under his breath. He was hot and hungry and if he never had to ask another pointless question about how many men had been on a boat, it would be too soon. Surely any decent spy would bring their *own* boat for a covert mission anyway!

Emily sped off down the coast road towards Castle Key, her long curls flying out behind her. She wasn't going to let Jack see the tears of frustration that were stinging her eyes. She'd been so sure that Mystery Man had been pushed off a boat. Maybe she was wrong. But what else did they have to go on?

Jack followed in his own personal cloud of grumpiness. Stretching away to the left, South Moor was an ocean of yellow gorse in flower, dotted with lambs on wobbly legs, their quavering bleats floating on the breeze, but neither Emily nor Jack was in the mood for scenery. The only one enjoying the ride was Drift; he sat up in his basket, the earthy scents of spring tickling his nose and the wind ruffling his ears. Bliss!

Jack was wondering whether they were going to stop for lunch any time soon, when he was overtaken by a camper van bristling with racks of surf boards and kayaks. Jack watched as it turned down a bumpy track to the right leaving the thumping beat of rock music in its wake.

A little way down the road Jack passed an even

narrower track. The old wooden signpost was so weathered and overgrown with wild flowers that you could barely see the words: *Keyhole Cove. Access on foot only. No vehicles.*

He braked so hard he almost somersaulted over the handlebars.

'Wait!' he yelled. 'I've had a brainwave!' How did Emily manage to cycle so fast, he wondered. Jack was a BMX champion (under thirteen, South-East Regional) and he still found it hard to catch her up.

Emily stood down from her pedals. A large proportion of Jack's brainwaves were either a) barking mad, or b) lunch-related. But every now and then he did come up with a lightning flash of pure genius.

Jack fishtailed to a halt beside her. 'That path goes down to Keyhole Cove, right?'

Emily nodded.

'So that last track we passed leads to the coast, just west of Keyhole Cove?'

'Yes. West Rock Beach. So?'

'Yesterday you said that from Pencarrick Point, you'd be washed eastward by the tide and end up on the headland. What if you fell in at West Rock Beach? Where would the tide carry you from there?'

'East, I guess . . .' Suddenly Emily saw what Jack was getting at. 'Of course! You might end up in Keyhole Cove. Maybe Mystery Man went in the water at West Rock Beach.' She gave a sheepish smile. 'I was so fixated on the boat theory, I didn't think of that.'

Jack shrugged. 'Don't worry. You can buy me lunch to show your appreciation for my brilliance!'

Emily laughed. 'It's a deal. *After* we go back and scope out West Rock Beach!'

Moments later Jack and Emily were jumping off their bikes in the small parking area on the low cliffs above West Rock Beach. The camper van had parked and several people were unloading equipment and carrying surf boards down the sandy path to the beach like a procession of giant ants.

Jack wandered across the car park towards the ruins of an old fisherman's cottage. They were very close to the edge.

'Careful over there!' one of the surfers shouted. 'It's a sheer drop. You could easily fall in.'

My theory in a nutshell, Jack thought.

'Look at this!' Emily called from the other side of the car park. Jack ran back to find her inspecting a silver Ford Focus.

'This car didn't pass us on the road.' Emily's voice crackled with excitement. 'So where's the driver? Down on the beach?'

Jack peered down at the beach below. There was nobody in sight. Then he ambled over to the camper van and lent a hand to a guy lifting his surf board down from the roof. 'Have you seen anyone else around up here?' he asked.

'Nope! We're the first ones here. *Ex-cell-ent!*'

As they watched the surfer jog down to the beach Emily grinned at Jack. They may not have found the Lost City of Atlantis, but they were definitely on to something!

Eight

Brainwaves All Around

Emily ran her finger along the bonnet. Just as she thought! The car was covered in a fine layer of sand and sea salt. And there were white splats on the paintwork where seagulls had mistaken it for a new toilet facility. 'This car has been here some time!'

'Like overnight, you mean?' Jack asked.

Emily nodded slowly. 'Definitely.'

Jack tried the handles. The car was locked, of course.

He peered inside. He wasn't sure what he was expecting to see: a dead body? A conveniently placed photo ID card? But the car was empty.

'It's a hire car.' Emily pointed to a sticker on the windscreen displaying the logo and phone number of Carrickstowe Car Hire. 'Now we just need to find out who hired it!'

'How?' Jack asked.

But Emily had already pulled out her mobile and started dialling. 'Excuse me,' she said. 'One of your cars is blocking my mum's car in. Could you give me the number of the person who hired it so we can call and ask them to come and move it?'

'Sorry, I can't give out that information.' Emily had switched the phone to speaker so Jack could hear the brisk voice at the other end of the line.

'Oh, no!' Emily sounded as if she was about to burst out crying. 'It's an emergency, because we've got to get to the hospital . . .'

'Hospital, you say? Alright, tell me the registration number, dear. I'll give the driver a call myself and ask him to move it.'

Emily ground her teeth in annoyance, but she read out the number from the licence plate.

'Hold on. I'll call him on the other line and come back to you.' There were several minutes of classical music before the lady from Carrickstowe Car Hire came back. 'For some reason Mr Novak's phone seems to be out of service. Tell me where you are, dear, and I'll send someone to move the car. We keep spare keys.'

'Actually, don't worry,' Emily said quickly. 'Mum's just managed to squeeze the car out. Thanks, bye!' She hung up and smiled triumphantly. 'Phew, I thought she was *never* going to give me a name!'

Jack shook his head in awe. 'If MI5 turns you down you could have a career on the stage. That was an Oscar-winning performance.' He mimicked Emily's panic-stricken voice. *'Oh, no, it's an emergency. We've got to get to the hospital!'*

'Well, it's true. It *is* an emergency. If we don't find out what's going on, Mystery Man could be in big trouble!'

Jack grinned. '*Mr Novak* could be in trouble, you mean!'

Emily nodded and walked cautiously towards the cliff edge. It was a little higher than Pencarrick Point and the rocks were closer – their peaks poking up through the waves like the fins of circling sharks – but if you were lucky and landed between the rocks, you could survive the fall, and quite possibly wash up in Keyhole Cove, just around the next point.

She tried to picture the sequence of events. Novak hired a car in Carrickstowe, drove to this remote spot and parked. Why? No doubt D. I. Hassan would say he came up here to think things over after a row with his wife, and accidentally slipped over the edge. But

Emily's suspicions were running along an entirely different track. Had Novak arranged to meet someone up here? The ruined cottage would be perfect for a secret rendezvous. *And had that someone pushed him off the cliff?*

Emily's thoughts were interrupted by a joyful bark from Drift. He was chasing the seagulls that had gathered to squabble over the litter in the corners of the ruins. It was a popular spot for walkers to shelter and eat a snack on a blustery hike along the coastal path. Suddenly Emily caught sight of something that stood out from the plastic bottles, crisp packets and sweet wrappers. A scrap of newspaper danced past Drift's paws. A seagull pecked at it, then decided it wasn't worth eating and shook it off its beak. Emily leaped and caught it in her hands before it could flutter away like a butterfly on the ocean breeze.

'What are you doing?' Jack shouted, pulling her away from the edge. 'This isn't the best place to start practising your kick-boxing moves!'

Emily laughed and held up her prize.

Jack stared at her. 'Random bit of old newspaper. Big deal!'

Emily sat on a crumbling wall and smoothed the piece of paper out on her knee.

> Unemployed plumber Steve Matlock (35) was sentenced today to three months for aggravated

burglary. Matlock, a long-term drug addict, has a string of previous convictions . . .

Emily turned the cutting over to find half an advert for a concert in Manchester City Gallery that had taken place two weeks ago.

Jack looked over her shoulder and shrugged. 'Like I said. Random.'

Maybe, Emily thought. But she didn't believe anything was random when it came to criminal investigations. This wasn't just a torn-off scrap of newspaper. Someone had cut neatly round the Steve Matlock story with scissors. She had no idea what the connection was between a burglar in Manchester and a drowning man in Cornwall, but she was sure there was one.

Emily sealed the newspaper cutting inside an evidence bag and dropped it in her satchel.

~

Meanwhile Scott was struggling to stay awake in the hospital café. He'd spotted a kid stealing biscuits from the counter, a nurse sneaking outside for a cigarette, and a cleaner sweeping dust under a doormat, but no one who looked like an international spy. But then, a real spy was hardly going to make it easy by roaring through the double doors in an Aston Martin, wearing a sharp suit and shades, to the accompaniment of the James Bond theme tune over the hospital tannoy system! Nurses, doctors, cleaners, workmen, visitors, patients, any one of them could be a cleverly disguised secret agent with a sawn-off shotgun concealed in their mop, bucket or wheelchair.

Secret agent? Oh, no, Scott thought. *Now* I'm *the one who's been spending too much time around Emily!*

He gave up playing Hunt the Spy and began scrolling through the playlist on his phone. He'd downloaded some old Splinter Planet tracks so he could practise the guitar parts. If he was going to have a jam session with Nick Dylan he needed to know their material so he didn't look like some kind of clueless newbie. He reclined in the squeaky vinyl seat and closed his eyes, losing himself in *Ready, Aim, Rock.* He imagined his guitar in his hands and could almost feel the strings under his fingers as he tackled a tricky chord change, then stormed through to the final majestic riff.

He felt a tap on his shoulder. He opened his eyes to see a Chinese lady leaning towards him from the next table. She tipped her head to one side and frowned with concern. 'Are you alright?'

Scott shrugged. 'Er, yeah. Fine. Why?'

'I just wondered,' the woman said nervously. 'You know, the twitching and the thrashing about and the wailing.'

Wailing? Scott thought. *What's she talking about?*

Then he felt himself blush. He must have got a bit carried away playing air guitar and – his blush deepened – had he really been singing along? *Out loud?* He sat up straight and tried to look unruffled. 'Sorry, I'm fine, really, absolutely fine.'

The lady smiled and turned away.

Scott flopped back on the seat until the hot prickles of humiliation died down. He bet things like this never happened to mega-successful musicians. One thing was for sure, it wouldn't happen to Flak Petersen. Scott pictured the ice-cool drummer in the black leather coat, reading about advanced mathematics and tapping out drum rhythms on the arm of his chair.

Suddenly Scott sprang up so fast he knocked his Coke flying.

He'd seen someone else tapping his fingers today – just like Flak Petersen!

Giving a double thumbs-up to the Chinese lady as he backed slowly out of the café, Scott pictured the drowning man sitting up in bed that morning. He had been cracking jokes, laughing nervously, and *tapping his fingers*! Scott had thought it was just a nervous tic, simply part of the stress of losing his memory, but what if Mystery Man was a drummer? It all made sense – the massive arm muscles, the back problems, the hearing loss. A professional drummer could have all those symptoms.

Scott knew he had to test his theory out.

Now all he needed was a drum kit!

Nine

Drum Solo

With the help of the friendly nurse, Penny Miller in A&E, Scott eventually tracked down a drum kit in a cupboard marked *Music Therapy* in one of the outpatient centres on the other side of hospital and got permission to borrow it. It turned out to be a junior-sized kit decorated with photographs of Take That. He lugged it up to Mystery Man's ward, cymbals crashing and snare drum rattling all the way. He felt like a one-man band.

Luckily, when he got to the ward, Nurse Redpath was on a break and Dr Obi was with the drowning man, checking his blood pressure. He was willing to give the drum test a try, and between them, Scott and the doctor set the kit up next to the bed. Mystery Man laughed and shook his head. He picked the drumsticks up and turned them over in his hands as if wondering whether to hold them like chopsticks or knitting needles. He tapped the sticks on the snare drum in an uncertain paradiddle, gradually gaining speed and volume. Suddenly, a look of recognition came over the man's face – as if he'd been trying to tune into a radio station in his head and had finally found a signal – and he broke into an electrifying drum solo!

The performance ended on a magnificent crescendo.

'Wow!' Scott exclaimed, the cymbal still ringing in his ears. 'That was awesome!'

Mystery Man grinned and rubbed his sore ribs. 'Well, I'll be! I have no idea where *that* came from!'

'I do!' The voice came from Harry Stiles, the frail old man on the other side of the ward. 'It was *Moby Dick* by John Bonham of Led Zeppelin. One of the greatest drum solos of all time. I saw Bonham play it live in 1968. He broke three pairs of sticks. Those were the days!'

Mystery Man grinned and picked up the sticks, but before he could play again, Nurse Redpath came steaming down the ward. 'What is this racket?' she demanded. 'This is a hospital, not a pop concert! And it's not even visiting time!' She glowered at Dr Obi, her face as sour as if she'd swallowed a hornet.

Scott looked up and saw two figures tiptoeing into the ward. Nurse Redpath swivelled round, her shoes squeaking, and was about to banish all visitors, when Dr Obi held up a hand and asked her to allow them two more minutes with the drowning man.

'The drum kit could be a breakthrough, the vital trigger to regaining his memory,' he explained.

Jack and Emily joined Scott and Dr Obi at the bedside.

'Guess what!' Scott crowed. 'He's a drummer!'

'Cool!' Jack said. 'But *we've* got something even better!' He turned to the man. 'Your name is Novak!' he announced with a flourish.

Jack waited for the big reaction. This was the moment of truth. Cue lights, cue music, cue dancing girls!

But the lights didn't so much as flicker. And the dancing girls didn't even leave the dressing room.

'What about Steve Matlock?' Emily asked desperately. 'Does *that* name mean anything?'

The man's face remained stubbornly blank.

Nurse Redpath tapped her watch. 'Your two minutes is up! Out! All of you!'

On the way back to the café, Scott explained that the surveillance operation had been a waste of time. 'There are so many people around, it's hopeless trying to pick out a potential spy. We really need to keep guard on the ward . . .'

'Fat chance of that with old Redpath on the warpath!' Jack laughed. But suddenly he had another of his brainwaves. 'I know! We'll recruit an undercover agent of our own. An insider!'

Before Scott and Emily could ask what he meant, Jack had sprinted to the shop in the concourse, bought a packet of wine gums as an advance payment and headed back to the ward. A few minutes later he returned, a big grin on his face.

'Mission accomplished! I sneaked in while Redpath was talking to another nurse. Harry Stiles is on the case! If he sees anyone suspicious he'll press his emergency button and Redpath will be on the warpath to see them off in nanoseconds.'

~

With Agent Stiles on Guard Duty on the ward, the friends relocated their HQ to one of Emily's many hideouts on Castle Key island – somewhere where the air was full of wild thyme and sea spray rather than disinfectant fumes and, more importantly, where Drift didn't have to wait outside.

The boys had never been to the enormous willow tree before. It grew on the bank of the little stream that ran into the sea from a spring near the old tin mine on North Moor. A lightning strike had split the ancient tree down the middle, but over the years the two halves had fused together to form a perfect circular room.

'Awesome!' Jack whistled as Drift led the way into the hollow tree. Rustling leaves formed a canopy over the open roof, dappling the light inside like leopard skin. The bulges on the inner wall of the gnarled tree trunk made perfect seats – all covered in bright green moss, as soft and springy as velvet cushions.

'Cool,' Scott said, climbing up inside the hollow to a hole that came out on a wide branch. 'You can see right across the moor to the causeway from here.'

Emily sat down and opened her notebook. She had a lot of important new information to add. Underneath the question *Who is the drowning man??????* she wrote *(1) drummer* and *(2) American*. Then she added a new heading, *Maybe*, and began a list.

Name = Novak?
Hire car abandoned at West Rock Beach?
Connection to Steve Matlock/Manchester?

'That's a lot of maybes,' Jack commented, breaking off from testing the emergency biscuits that Emily had stashed in a little niche in the trunk – inside an old tin to thwart raids by hungry squirrels.

'So, what's an American drummer doing in Castle Key?' Emily wondered, chewing on her pen.

Scott climbed down from the observation branch. 'He's a musician. There's a music festival at Castle Key. Join the dots!'

'Of course!' Emily said. 'We just have to ask around all the bands who are rehearsing up at the castle.'

Jack snorted. 'Ask what? *Excuse me, have any of you guys mislaid your drummer?* You'd think they'd have noticed by now! It's not like losing your bus pass or something.'

Emily frowned. 'Not if the other band members were meant to be meeting him here. They might just think he got delayed on the way. We can show people the photo I took of him on my phone this morning. We'll see if anyone recognizes him – or the name Novak.'

Scott grinned. *Hanging around the rehearsals chatting to the musicians in all the bands?* This was his kind of investigation!

Ten

Festivals and Flying Kangaroos

The scene in the castle grounds was chaotic. There were even more people milling around and shouting at each other than when the film crew had come to shoot scenes for the Agent Diamond movie last summer. Probably even more than when the castle had last been invaded by an enemy army in 1385.

The main stage had been built on the grassy area

that had once been the moat in front of the castle, with the ruined towers behind as a backdrop. There were engineers everywhere, checking out the sound and lighting systems. Musicians hurried from place to place, carrying guitars or microphones, while roadies lugged amplifiers and reels of cable. Tents and marquees had been erected all around the site, serving as dressing rooms and stages. Enticing smells of hot dogs, crêpes and pizza were already wafting from the refreshment stalls. The friends spotted Dotty from the seafront café setting up a stand selling Cornish pasties, and Colin Warnock, the purple-haired curate from St Michael's church, helping to marshal the crowds who were already arriving to stake out a good spot ahead of the opening performance that evening. Over the hubbub of excited chatter, music pumped out from every direction.

Scott thought he must have died and gone to heaven!

'It's a good thing that Mrs Loveday is away on her Caribbean cruise,' Emily laughed. 'Imagine what she'd make of this.'

'About the same as the Caribbean people are making of Mrs Loveday!' Jack muttered. Mrs Loveday, Castle Key's official gossip queen, was his sworn enemy.

The friends covered every inch of the festival site, asking all musicians if they were missing a drummer. There were several false alarms. It seemed that drummers were notorious for wandering off and going AWOL, although they usually turned up at the bar at the Ship and Anchor. None of them looked like the photograph of Mystery Man or answered to the name of Novak. Just when he was about to give up, Scott spotted the members of Splinter Planet gathered near the main stage, waiting to go on for a sound check.

'There's no point asking them,' Jack said. 'We know they've got their drummer. You could hardly miss Flak Petersen.'

'But they might recognize our guy from another band,' Emily pointed out. 'He's about the same age.' She ducked under the rope, past the sign that said PERFORMERS ONLY, and slipped past two large bouncers. Drift and the boys followed.

Flak Petersen acknowledged the friends with a half smile. When Scott explained they were looking for a missing drummer, possibly named Novak, he closed his eyes and swayed a little as if dancing to a tune only he could hear. He gave the photo on Emily's phone a long stare, and even turned it upside-down to see it from all angles. Scott held his breath. Were they on to something?

But finally Flak shook his head. 'Sorry, man, I'm not getting any vibes here.'

Billy Riordan snatched the phone. 'Give us a look at that now, will you?' He glanced at the photo, swore, and then thrust the phone back at Emily. 'Never laid eyes on the fella.'

Nick Dylan was nowhere to be seen but Lauren, looking very pretty in a short white dress, cowboy boots and a straw hat, was sitting on a deck chair reading a fashion magazine. She shrugged when Emily showed her the photo of Mystery Man. 'No, I don't recognize him.'

'Where's Nick?' Emily asked. 'Maybe we could ask him.'

Lauren gestured with her thumb to a tent behind a screen. 'Nick can't be disturbed now. He's meditating. Give me the phone and I'll show him in a minute.'

Reluctantly Emily handed over the phone and Lauren disappeared behind the screen.

Scott peeped through a gap in the tent. Nick Dylan, wearing red and black skinny jeans and a purple t-shirt with the sleeves cut out, was lounging on an inflatable armchair. The meditating appeared to consist of working his way through a packet of peanut M&M's, and – for a moment Scott thought his eyes were deceiving him – *knitting*! The needles were clicking away and a stripy scarf was hanging from his side like a tail. *Knitting*? That was so uncool it was almost cool again.

Scott watched as, true to her word, Lauren tapped Nick on the shoulder, quietly asked him a question and waved Emily's phone under his nose. Nick frowned at it and shook his head.

Lauren returned the phone to Emily. 'Sorry, Nick says he's never seen this guy.'

'Maybe we're on the wrong track here,' Jack said, heading for the refreshment stands. Investigating was hungry work, especially when you were getting precisely nowhere.

Sitting on the grass, leaning against the wall of a tower, the friends munched on their pasties, feeding pieces to a very eager Drift. Emily's dad hurried by with two safety officers, discussing the barriers that had been installed to stop anyone wandering too close to the cliffs. Suddenly Emily had an idea. Dad had been in the music business a long time. Maybe *he* would recognize their mystery man. She ran after him. Jack and Scott shrugged and followed her.

Seth Wild glanced down at the phone and ran his fingers through his long grey ponytail. 'Novak, you say? Name doesn't ring a bell. You could try looking through my old albums at home to see if you can find him there.'

'Why would he be in your photo albums?' Jack asked, confused.

Seth Wild laughed. 'Not photo albums! Records. Those round black vinyl things we used to play music on in the olden days. The record sleeves always list the names of the musicians . . .'

Emily grinned. 'Dad, you're a genius!'

~

Half an hour later, the friends were sitting in the family living room on the second floor of The Lighthouse, surrounded by piles of old records. There was only one more shelf to go and they'd still not found the man they were looking for. But at least it had been fun. They'd rolled around laughing at the bizarre names of the bands, the freaky fashions, and the hysterical hairstyles so much that Jack thought he might actually have done some permanent damage to his rib cage.

'Look at this one!' he spluttered, holding up an album with a picture of three men with long bouffant 1970s hairdos flying over the London skyline, chased by a herd of sinister, winged kangaroos.

'Hang on!' Emily cried, lunging for the record. 'That could be him!' She blocked off the flowing brown hair and focused on the face, holding up the photo on her phone next to it. 'I'm sure of it. Look, he's got the same deep-set eyes and crooked nose.'

Scott examined the album cover. Emily was right. The figure soaring over Big Ben, riding on a giant drumstick, definitely looked like the drowning man.

But that wasn't even the spookiest part.

The other two musicians, using their guitars as flying broomsticks, were Nick Dylan and Billy Riordan.

The album was by Splinter Planet.

Eleven

Rock History

Scott held up the album. 'This is so weird!'

'I know,' Jack shuddered. 'Those flying kangaroos are going to give me nightmares!'

'Not the *kangaroos*!' Emily laughed. Sometimes Jack really needed to try to keep up. 'This guy is definitely our mystery man. Which means that he was once the drummer with Splinter Planet. But the entire band just told us to our faces that they'd never seen him before in their lives. Why did they lie to us?'

'Maybe they didn't recognize him?' Jack suggested. 'He has changed a bit since . . .' he checked the date on the record. '. . . 1973. He doesn't have all that hair now for a start.'

Scott shook his head. 'Uh-uh! They'd have to be blind not to recognize him. His face has hardly changed. And anyway, we told them his name as well.' Scott turned the record over and started scanning through the list of band members, producers and other contributors, but to his surprise, there was no one called Novak. 'Drums: Ronnie Brandon,' he read aloud. He stared at the name and back at the photo on Emily's phone once more. 'This drummer guy is *definitely* the man sitting in the hospital bed in Carrickstowe. It seems Mystery Man must be called Ronnie Brandon.'

Emily took another look at the album cover and had to agree. 'So, the Novak guy who hired that car and abandoned it on the cliffs at West Rock Beach must be a red herring, nothing to do with this case after all.' Although she was disappointed that her brilliant clue hadn't panned out, she was excited they'd finally discovered Mystery Man's real identity.

Scott thought for a moment. 'Unless you heard the name wrong, Em? Maybe the woman at the hire company said *Brandon*?'

Emily laughed. 'No way. Novak? Brandon? They're

not exactly alike. I'd have to be as deaf as a drummer to get those two mixed up!'

Scott nodded thoughtfully.

Jack looked from Scott to Emily. 'OK, tell me if I'm being a bit slow here, but isn't *Flak Petersen* the drummer with Splinter Planet? Where does this Ronnie Brandon guy fit in?'

'Maybe he's like the fifth Beatle!' Scott suggested.

Jack shook his head. 'No, that's not making it any clearer.'

Scott laughed. 'You really don't know your rock history, do you? The original drummer with the Beatles was this guy called Pete Best, but he was replaced early on by Ringo Starr, and now hardly anyone remembers Pete Best was in the band first.'

'Yeah, that sounds about right.' Emily sorted through a pile of records. 'These are the rest of Splinter Planet's albums. The next one came out in 1975. The drummer is Flak Petersen.' She turned the cover round to show the boys. It featured a stylish black-and-white shot of the band playing a game of chess. Flak Petersen obviously had no truck with airborne kangaroos!

'So,' Scott said, slowly spelling out his thoughts. 'Some time between 1973 and 1975, Ronnie Brandon leaves Splinter Planet. And now, over thirty years later, he turns up, half drowned, only a mile or two away from where his old band are preparing for their big reunion concert.'

Emily was scribbling furiously in her notebook. 'And all his old band mates deny ever having seen him before!'

'Fishy and getting fishier,' Jack commented.

'And then there's the puzzle of *It wasn't Chris!*' Emily added. 'Ronnie Brandon kept saying those words, but I've looked through all the producers and technicians and backing singers listed on these albums, and there isn't a single Chris anywhere. Who is the mysterious Chris?'

'To the internet!' Scott shouted, leaping off the sofa.

But at that moment Emily's mum called up the stairs. 'Emily! Can you help me with the laundry?'

Scott grinned. 'Shame – I was just leaving to do some vital internet research on Ronnie Brandon. But I'm sure Jack won't mind helping.'

Jack made a dash for the door. 'I'd better come with you. What if you're attacked by flying kangaroos?'

'I think I've got it covered,' Scott laughed.

Emily grinned. 'Thanks, Jack! I'm sure you're an expert at folding sheets!'

~

Scott settled down at a computer in the small Castle Key library. The internet connection here was much faster than using his phone. He typed RONNIE BRANDON into the search box and pored over the results.

What he found threw up a lot of answers.

And a lot of questions too.

Scott read an article dated January 1975, which said:

In a shock press-release today, Ronnie Brandon has confirmed he is leaving Splinter Planet. Asked why he was quitting the band, Brandon told our interviewer the split was due to 'musical differences'. Guitarist/lead singer Dylan and bass player Riordan denied rumours that the break-up was triggered by last year's tragic road accident.

Tragic road accident? That would explain the old scars on the drowning man's arms, Scott thought. He searched the news archives for information about the crash and found it in an American news report from 1974.

Members of the popular rock band Splinter Planet are recovering in hospital tonight after their tour bus was involved in a late-night freeway smash. Nick Dylan and Billy Riordan are thought to have suffered minor injuries while drummer, Ronnie Brandon, has been more seriously hurt. Two passengers were killed in a second vehicle involved in the accident. The driver of Splinter Planet's tour bus, a member of the band's road crew, was also found dead at the scene. He leaves behind a wife and four-year-old son in Manchester, England.

Scott stared at the words on the screen. Memories flooded back. His mother had been killed in a car crash and he'd been four at the time, too. People thought he was too young to understand what had happened, but he'd heard them talking about it from his bedroom, where he'd been sent with a kind policewoman to play with Lego. His imagination had filled in the rest. Scott pushed the memories away. They were too sharp, too painful. He had to focus on the investigation at hand.

He made himself read the last sentence of the article.

The driver has been named as Chris Castelli.

It wasn't Chris! Suddenly the drowning man's words were ringing in Scott's ears again.

He knew that the most significant breakthrough in the entire case was staring him in the face.

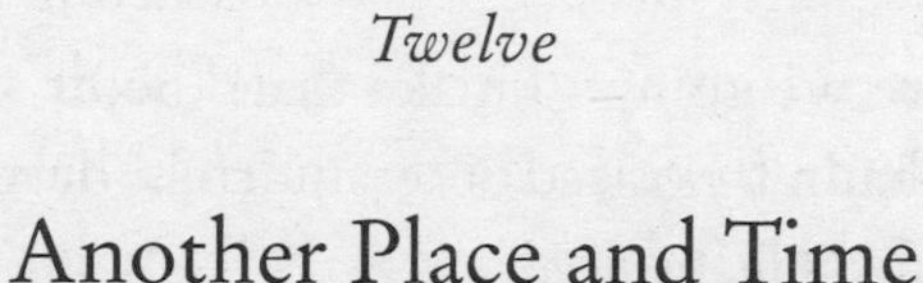

Twelve

Another Place and Time

The weather had turned much cooler overnight, spring sunshine giving way to sky the colour of old tin cans. So when Emily called the boys at Stone Cottage to arrange a summit meeting at the hollow tree HQ next morning, Jack made sure he packed his cold-weather survival rations before they set off on their bikes.

'Instant hot chocolate!' he announced, pulling a tin

out of his rucksack as soon as they were inside the tree trunk.

'How are we going to make that?' Scott scoffed. 'In case you hadn't noticed, the squirrels don't seem to have installed electricity.'

Jack stuck his tongue out and pulled a camping kettle from the bag. 'We make a fire, of course. We can take water from the stream. Look, I've even brought marshmallows!'

'Just a minor detail, but won't a fire burn down the tree?' Scott pointed out.

Emily smiled. 'It'll be OK as long as we keep the fire small. We can contain it with stones. There are lots of good flat ones on the stream bed.'

Before long the friends had constructed a fire pit and gathered supplies of dry grass and twigs. Emily set a spark to the kindling using the fire-lighting kit she always kept in her satchel. Soon the kettle was steaming on a hot stone, and crumpets – also from the bottomless food supply in Jack's backpack – were toasting on the ends of long sticks. Drift stretched out comfortably on the soft mat of leaf mulch by the fire. The little room inside the hollow tree couldn't have been cosier if it had had central heating and wall-to-wall carpets.

'So,' Emily asked Scott, 'what did you come up with on Ronnie Brandon?'

Scott stirred his hot chocolate and smiled mysteriously.

Jack was bursting with impatience; infuriatingly,

Scott had refused to reveal the results of yesterday's internet searches until they were all together to 'discuss it properly'.

Scott cleared his throat. 'As we know, Ronnie Brandon was the original drummer with Splinter Planet. He made two albums with them before leaving in 1975. According to this report in *Melody Maker* magazine – ' Scott held up a print-out of the article – 'the split was due to "musical differences". Flak Petersen joined a few months later and the band went on to enjoy a meteoric rise to stardom. However, there may have been more to the break-up than meets the eye . . .' Scott paused for dramatic effect.

'Go on, the suspense is killing me!' Jack tried to sound sarcastic, but actually it nearly was.

'Ronnie and the rest of the band were involved in a crash in their tour bus a few months before Ronnie left the band. The driver of the bus was killed. He was a roadie, and his name was . . . wait for it . . . Chris Castelli.'

Emily's eyes glowed in the firelight. '*Chris* Castelli?'

'Chris as in "It wasn't Chris"?' Jack asked. 'As in the almost-last words of the half-drowned Ronnie Brandon?'

'Exactly!' Scott said.

'So what was Ronnie going on about?' Jack groaned. 'It's *obvious* this Chris Castelli can't have had anything to do with Ronnie ending up swimming with the fishes.

The guy's been dead for thirty years. Unless of course he's come back from the grave. *I am the phantom roadie!*' Jack wailed, doing his best ghost impression. He noticed Emily frowning. 'Oops, sorry, Em, am I scaring you?' Ever since Emily had been seriously spooked by the midnight ghost during Operation Lost Star, Jack had teased her about being afraid of ghosts.

'I'm not *frightened*!' Emily poked Jack with her toasting stick. 'I'm just trying to figure out what Ronnie Brandon meant by *It wasn't Chris*. He said it twice. He must have been trying to tell us *something* important.'

Scott nodded. 'Actually, I have a theory . . .'

'Anyone want butter or jam on their crumpets?' Jack asked.

'What else have you got in that bag?' Emily giggled. 'Roast beef? Banoffee pie?'

Scott sighed. 'Hello? Anyone interested in hearing my theory?'

'We're all ears!' Jack said.

'The newspaper report says that Chris Castelli had a four-year-old son at the time of the accident. Well, he'd be in his thirties now. That's the same age as the burglar from Manchester in that newspaper clipping you found at West Rock Beach.'

Emily looked up, her knife hovering midway between a jar of Aunt Kate's homemade raspberry jam and a crumpet. 'You're saying Steve Matlock is Chris Castelli's *son*?'

'Yeah, he could easily have changed his name.'

'That's stretching it a bit!' Jack snorted. 'They're the same age therefore they must be the same person. On that logic, Emily and I are the same person because we're both twelve!'

Scott laughed. 'Actually, it's not stretching it as much as you think.' Scott tapped the news report. 'It says here that Chris Castelli was from Manchester, England. That's the same city as Steve Matlock.'

Jack was still not looking convinced, but Scott had saved his trump card for last. He held up a second print-out.

'And then there's this! I found out some more background stuff about Ronnie in an old interview he gave while he was still with Splinter Planet. Ronnie Brandon married in 1972. His wife was called Rosa *Novak*.'

'The Rosa tattoo!' Emily cried. 'That proves beyond doubt that Mystery Man is Ronnie Brandon. Rosa is his wife.'

'And,' Scott explained, 'it also means that the car you saw up at West Rock Beach was almost certainly left there by Ronnie. He just used his wife's name when he hired it. Ronnie Brandon is Mr Novak! Which means it's quite possible that he's the one who dropped that newspaper clipping, linking him to Steve Matlock.'

Emily was writing in her notebook so fast that sparks

were practically flying from her pen. 'Steve Matlock is now officially our prime suspect!' she said.

'Never mind, Em!' Jack said in a sympathetic voice.

'What?' she asked.

'Looks like this case has nothing to do with spies, after all.'

Emily ignored the teasing as she filed Scott's printouts neatly in the back of her notebook. But suddenly a worrying thought crossed her mind. 'If this Steve Matlock guy is coming after Ronnie Brandon because he blames him for his father's death or something, maybe he has it in for the other band members who were in the crash too. Nick Dylan and Billy Riordan could be in danger!'

Scott nodded and then checked his watch. 'It's visiting time. Let's put this fire out and go and see whether any of this new information jogs Mystery Man's memory.'

'Hi Ronnie,' Scott called. 'Ronnie Brandon?'

Mystery Man was sitting up in bed watching TV. He whipped round at the sound of Scott's voice. He looked surprised, furrowing his brows above his deep-set eyes, squinting as if trying to make out a figure in the distance.

'Wh . . . what did you call me?' he asked.

'Ronnie,' Emily said. 'You're Ronnie Brandon.'

'You used to be the drummer with Splinter Planet,' Jack chipped in.

Scott pressed a button on his iPhone and began to play one of the early Splinter Planet tracks on the mini speaker. As if in a trance, the man picked up the drumsticks and began to play along on the kit still set up by the side of the bed. Scott switched the music off. The man continued to play without missing a beat. At the end of the piece he stared at the kit in silence for a long moment, then looked to the side as if hearing a voice in his ear. Suddenly he clutched his head, his face contorted as if in agony.

'Ronnie?' Scott asked. 'Are you OK?'

The man flopped back against the pillow. 'It wasn't Chris!' he sobbed.

'What wasn't Chris?' Emily asked gently.

'They blamed it on Chris. But it wasn't him!'

'Blamed him for what?' Scott prompted.

But suddenly Jack knew what Ronnie was talking about. 'You mean Chris Castelli wasn't driving the tour bus when it crashed?'

Ronnie's hands dropped to his sides. He stared at Jack, but his gaze was fixed as if he were seeing something altogether different projected onto the place where Jack stood. A terrible scene from another place and time.

Thirteen

Despicable!

Emily perched on the edge of Ronnie's bed. 'Can you remember what happened?' she asked gently.

Ronnie nodded. 'It's late at night.' He stared straight ahead as if seeing the whole scene play out on a movie screen. 'We've played a gig in Chicago. There was a big party after the show. We're all in the tour bus, driving to the next town. We've been on tour for months. It's a different town every night. We're speeding down the freeway like there's no tomorrow, a big row going on about the tracks for the next album. All of a sudden, we're hurtling out of control, skidding across the lanes. The bus is rolling over and we're being thrown about like balls in a lottery machine. The screech of metal, the smell of burning rubber, Billy swearing at the top of his voice . . . then it's all quiet. Too quiet.' Ronnie shuddered. When he continued, his voice was barely more than a whisper. 'He'd taken a bend too fast and smashed head-on into a car coming the other way.'

'Who had?' Jack demanded impatiently. 'Who was driving?'

'Nick. It was Nick Dylan.'

'Nick?' Scott staggered back from the bed as if Ronnie had landed an uppercut on his jaw. Nick Dylan was one of his all-time heroes . . .

'So how come everyone thought it was this Chris Castelli guy?' Emily asked.

Ronnie sighed. 'It was a cover-up. Nick was the golden boy of the band. He was also very drunk. Two people lost their lives in the other car. If the story got out that Nick was driving, the band would have been over. Chris Castelli was one of our road crew. He'd been riding shotgun with Nick, reading the map. He was killed instantly.' Ronnie shook his head. 'Billy Riordan and Nick figured that since Chris was dead anyway, it wouldn't make any difference to him if they said *he* was the one driving . . .'

'But that's terrible!' Emily cut in. 'It's . . .' she searched for the right word. 'It's despicable.'

'And what about you?' Jack asked. 'Were you in on the cover-up?'

'Not at first. I was badly injured but I managed to crawl out of the back of the bus seconds before it went up like fireworks on the fourth of July. The paramedics found me unconscious on the road. When I came round in hospital, Nick and Billy were at my bedside. I thought they were concerned about me, but they just wanted to make sure I'd play along with their story. When I refused, they offered me money to keep my mouth shut. In the end I agreed.' Ronnie looked down at his hands. 'It's not something I'm proud of, but Billy can be very persuasive. And Nick was only nineteen. I didn't want to wreck his life by going public. But after that I didn't want anything more to do with either of them. I left the band and moved back to America with Rosa. We bought a ranch in Texas . . .'

'A ranch? So you're a cowboy!' Jack was thrilled. A cowboy was way more exciting than a road worker, or even a spy.

'Sure am!' Ronnie smiled for the first time since he'd regained his memory. 'I still play drums in a local folk band, but mostly I'm out working with the cattle.'

'And you changed your name to Novak?' Emily asked.

Ronnie nodded. 'I wanted to leave everything about

my life with Splinter Planet behind, so I adopted Rosa's surname.'

Jack grinned. 'I think the feeling was mutual. When we showed the band your picture, they pretended they didn't know you!'

'How's our patient today?'

Emily, Scott, Jack and Ronnie all looked round as Dr Obi approached, tugging on the ends of the stethoscope round his neck.

'Quite remarkable!' he exclaimed, as the friends recounted how Ronnie's memory was coming back. The doctor's bloodshot eyes lit up with excitement. 'I'll have to write up this case for publication in the medical journals!'

Emily checked her watch. Dr Obi might be interested in the *medical* case, but she had a *criminal* case to solve, and visiting time was almost over. 'So why did you come to Castle Key?' she asked Ronnie.

'Was it to see Splinter Planet?' Scott had finally regained the power of speech after the Nick-was-driving body blow.

'Yeah. In a way. Ever since the crash, I've felt terrible about how Nick and Billy stitched Chris up. Chris was a great guy, but after the accident the media made out he was this party-animal drunk-driver who caused the deaths of the two innocent people in the other car. Think how that must have felt for his family! He had this little boy, only about four . . .'

'Steve?' Emily prompted.

Ronnie stared at her in astonishment. 'Yeah, that's right. But I don't know how you kids have found all this out. You should be working for the FBI.'

Emily beamed at him, glowing with the praise. *If she hadn't already set her sights on MI5,* Scott thought, *she'd probably emigrate to the USA, just so she could sign up for the FBI!*

'I kept in touch with Chris's family for a while,' Ronnie went on. 'Steve never got over his father's death. He went off the rails . . . drink, drugs. He had a tough time growing up, with everyone saying his dad was some kind of monster. He used his mother's name, Matlock, instead of Castelli, but people still found out who he was.' Ronnie took a drink of water from the glass on his bedside table. 'Anyway, a couple weeks back I read that Steve had been sent to jail for burglary. Not two minutes later I heard on MTV that Splinter Planet were all set to play a massive reunion gig to promote their new album. That's when I knew I couldn't keep quiet about the accident any longer. It just didn't seem right.'

Jack exchanged grins with Scott. Emily was practically jumping up and down on the bed in her eagerness to say what happened next. She was making those little *ooh* noises that the ultra-brainy girls at school made when they put their hands up to answer every single question.

'You arranged to meet Nick Dylan at West Rock Beach,' Emily said, 'and he hit you over the head and pushed you off the cliffs to stop you telling the world what really happened in that car crash!'

Ronnie screwed up his eyes as if trying to do long division in his head. 'Thing is, I can't remember anything after I left America to come here. It's like it's all hiding in the shadows, just out of reach . . . I remember sending Nick an email saying we had to meet. I wanted to give him one last chance to do the honourable thing and admit in public that he was driving the tour bus that night. If he refused to confess, I was going to reveal the whole story to the papers the day before their comeback concert. Nick emailed back, agreeing it was time to come clean, but he wanted to talk it over first. So we arranged to meet in Castle Key. I told Rosa I had to come to the UK on some business to do with the ranch and booked my flights . . .' Ronnie broke off. 'And from then on in, it all gets hazy.'

'So you don't remember hiring a car, driving to West Rock Beach and meeting Nick on the cliff?' Jack asked.

Ronnie shook his head.

Jack groaned. He couldn't believe they had ninety-nine per cent of the story, but were still missing the crucial final scene. It was worse than when Dad came in and turned the TV off five minutes before the end of a movie, just because there was school in the morning.

'Don't worry,' Dr Obi told Ronnie in a reassuring voice. 'If you just relax, those memories may well come back to you. It's quite usual for the period right around the trauma to remain a blank for longer.'

As they were preparing to leave, Emily was suddenly struck by a thought. Why had Nick Dylan taken Ronnie's threat to go public seriously? After all, it was only Ronnie's word against his that Nick was driving. Surely people would assume Ronnie had just come out of the woodwork to cash in on the band's new album. *Unless . . .*

'Ronnie?' she asked. 'Do you have *proof* that Nick was driving?'

Ronnie looked puzzled for a moment, but then he smiled. 'Yes! Of course! A tape. When Nick and Billy first offered me hush money to keep quiet about the crash, I was so furious with them that I taped the whole conversation. I've kept the tape all these years. I was going to offer to destroy it once Nick had come clean.'

'Where's that tape now?' Jack asked.

Ronnie shrugged. 'I don't remember. But I think I brought it with me to Castle Key.'

'I bet Nick nicked it off you on the cliff,' Jack said.

'Which means there's no way of proving he was the driver and clearing Chris's name any more,' Emily sighed.

Scott frowned. 'Maybe, but if Ronnie had any sense he'd have left the tape locked up safely until he knew

Nick had gone through with his side of the bargain and ’fessed up. It could be in your hotel room. Where were you staying?’

Ronnie shrugged. Sorry, I don’t remember.’

‘Visiting time was over three minutes ago.’ The shout came from Nurse Redpath. Her hair was scraped so tightly into its bun that her face looked like a mask. ‘Skedaddle! The lot of you!’ she ordered.

The friends passed Harry Stiles’s bed on the way out. Propped up on a bank of pillows, the old man was looking a lot stronger today.

‘Any suspicious visitors to report?’ Jack asked.

Harry rolled his eyes. ‘No, worse luck! I’ve been itching to ring the emergency button and get Attila the Bun in a tizzy!’

‘So who was that, then?’ Jack pointed to a middle-aged woman with greying hair and thick glasses. He’d noticed her sitting talking to Harry while they were with Ronnie Brandon, but she was now click-clacking out of the ward in her sensible, low-heeled court shoes, a bulging briefcase in her hand and a clipboard clutched to her chest.

‘Social worker,’ Harry said with a grin. ‘Asking me about my “arrangements” for when I leave this pleasure dome.’

‘Are you sure she was genuine?’ Emily demanded.

‘Oh, yes, she had one of those hospital ID badges round her neck. I told her I was planning to check into the penthouse at The Ritz for a few weeks,' Harry chuckled, 'before I head back to my luxury yacht on the French Riviera.'

The friends all laughed, but they stopped when Ronnie Brandon called from across the ward.

'Hey, kids! Something else just came back to me . . .'

Fourteen

A Time Bomb Ticking

But it was too late. Nurse Redpath had already sighted the friends heading back towards Ronnie's bed. She lasered them to the spot with her piercing blue eyes.

'If you lot don't leave immediately I will have no option but to call hospital security,' she warned.

Emily felt a stab of panic. There was no way she could leave without finding out what Ronnie had remembered. Frantically she searched for a way to distract the stern nurse's attention. Suddenly, as if reading her mind, Harry Stiles broke into a gurgling coughing fit. Worried that the old man was in distress, Emily spun round. Then she saw him wink at her.

Nurse Redpath bustled over to Harry's bed. 'Mr Stiles, what have I told you about over-exerting yourself?'

'Harry's OK,' Emily whispered to the boys. 'He's putting it on.' Using all her stealth skills, Emily sneaked back to Ronnie's side. 'Quick, tell me!' she hissed.

'I don't know if it means anything, but when I try to remember where I was staying, I just keep seeing this image of a soldier walking past my window. Maybe I'm imagining it . . .'

'OUT!' Nurse Redpath was back.

The friends fled, pausing only to flash a thumbs-up to Harry as they passed.

~

Scott, Jack and Emily gathered round a small table in the hospital café to plan their next move.

'Brilliant! So now we're looking for a hotel somewhere in Cornwall that a soldier might possibly have walked past some time in the last week,' Jack grumbled, when

Emily passed on what Ronnie had said. 'That's nearly as bad as *It wasn't Chris.* If there was an award for coming up with totally useless clues, old Ronnie Brandon would win every time!'

Scott ground his teeth. 'It's just so frustrating. If we could find the hotel, we might have a chance of getting hold of that tape and proving Ronnie's story.'

'I know,' Emily groaned. 'And until we do, Ronnie's still in danger. When Nick Dylan finds out that Ronnie's memory is coming back, he'll know that Ronnie could talk to the press at any moment about what really happened in that crash – not to mention tell the police that Nick pushed him off the cliff. Nick will have no option but to try to finish the job and silence Ronnie for good.'

Scott nodded grimly. 'It's like there's a time bomb ticking.'

Come on, think! Emily screamed at herself. *We have to be able to figure out where Ronnie was staying!* But there were no army barracks or military bases anywhere near Carrickstowe. Where could he have seen a soldier through his hotel window?

'Ronnie definitely said the soldier was *walking* past,' Scott murmured, thinking aloud. 'So his room must have been on the ground floor. That's unusual for a hotel.'

Jack grinned. 'Unless this soldier was on stilts. Or maybe he was cruising past on one of those flying kangaroos! I guess you could use the pouch for your ammo and—'

Emily banged her palms down on the table. 'That's it!'

'Flying kangaroos?' the boys echoed.

Emily laughed. 'No, it's the Grand Vista! That big, posh hotel on the seafront in Tregower. You know what's right outside it, don't you?'

Scott wasn't sure where Emily was going with this but he closed his eyes obediently and pictured the seafront in the little hamlet on the north-west coast of Castle Key island. 'Some fancy palm trees, a bandstand, a big statue . . . is it a king or a queen . . . no, it's a war memorial.'

'Exactly! Emily cried. 'There's a statue of a soldier returning from the First World War. He's on top of this really tall stone column. So . . . if you had a room at the front of the hotel you could look out of the window and he'd be right there in front of you!'

Jack mugged a mock-tragic face and then grinned. 'And I was so looking forward to tracking down a squadron of heavily armed airborne marsupials.'

~

The friends hatched their plan in record time. Emily and Jack would cycle to Tregower to find out whether Ronnie had stayed at the Grand Vista Hotel.

If he had, they'd try to gain access to his room and search for the tape. Meanwhile, Scott would return to the festival to keep tabs on Nick Dylan. Even though he really wanted to take part in the hotel quest, Scott had to admit that being a guitar-hero-worshipping fan gave him the perfect cover story for hanging around and stalking Nick's every move. And if Nick showed any sign of heading for the hospital, Scott would call the police and alert them that Ronnie Brandon's life was in danger.

'Operation Drowning Man is go!' Jack proclaimed, as they burst out through the double doors.

Sitting in his basket, guarding the bikes and helmets, Drift heard the friends race out of the hospital. *At last!* Much as he took his duties as Emily's Right Hand Dog seriously, he was starting to get just the teensiest bit fed up of sitting around outside the hospital on Lookout Duty. He didn't like the smell of the place, and the ambulance sirens set his hackles on edge. He gazed up with his ears on standby, hoping Emily had a more interesting mission in store.

Emily ruffled Drift's fur and was about to cycle off when she hesitated. The Grand Vista Hotel was far too posh to allow dogs inside. Was it really fair to ask Drift to do another shift outside on his own? She looked at Drift and then at Scott. *Drift and I go everywhere together*. But she couldn't deny he'd be much happier running around at the festival.

‘Scott,’ she said. ‘Do you think you could fit Drift’s basket on the back of your bike?’

Scott did a double-take. Was he hearing things? Did Emily just ask him to look after Drift? He couldn’t have felt more honoured if she’d pinned the George Cross on his t-shirt.

‘Sure, I’ll take care of him.’

Emily whispered a few words to Drift. Drift flicked his spotted ear in a salute. If Emily needed him to look after Scott for the afternoon, he was happy to accept the mission.

Emily gulped, then pedalled away before she could change her mind.

~

Scott spotted Nick Dylan sitting alone in one of the rehearsal tents near the castle, watching an old horror movie on a TV screen rigged up in the corner. Checking that Drift was close behind – he was taking his dog-watching responsibilities very seriously – he strolled in, pretending to be looking for Jack and Emily.

‘Sorry, mate, not seen them,’ Nick replied, hurriedly stuffing his knitting needles and half-finished scarf under his chair. ‘It’s like a ghost ship round here. Flak’s gone for a run, Lauren’s gone shopping in Carrickstowe, and Billy’s disappeared without trace too.’ Nick took a guitar from the case propped against his chair. 'You're the guy who plays guitar, aren't you?' he asked. 'Fancy a jam? I can teach you some of the tracks off our new album if you like.'

Scott shuffled his feet, suddenly struck with shyness. 'Wow, that'd be great,' he mumbled, 'but I don't have my guitar with me.'

'Here, use this. My spare.' Nick fetched a second guitar and pressed it into Scott's hands. 'OK, let's tune up.'

Drift shot under the chair as feedback squealed from the amplifiers. Scott quickly turned the sound down and made sure that Drift was OK among the balls of wool.

They warmed up with some old classics then started on the new tracks. But as they played, Scott's conscience was tying itself in knots. This was his dream come true: a one-to-one masterclass with a guitar god! He should be having the time of his life. And yet, how could he like and admire someone who'd passed the blame for a terrible accident onto an innocent man?

And yet Nick Dylan was acting so *normal* – well, as normal as an ageing rock star in leather jeans, zebra-striped waistcoat and a mane of dyed blond ringlets was ever going to get. He certainly didn't have the air of a man who'd thrown an old friend off a cliff a couple of days ago. If Nick was plotting to kill Ronnie to prevent him revealing his dark, despicable past, he certainly wasn't showing it. He seemed more concerned about people discovering his secret knitting habit!

Maybe Nick was just a super-cool customer who thought he'd got away with his crimes? *Or,* Scott wondered, *could we have got it all wrong?* Perhaps Ronnie's memories had got jumbled up somehow and Nick *wasn't* driving the tour bus on the night it crashed, after all? And perhaps Nick *hadn't* gone to meet Ronnie at West Rock Beach. What if someone else had pushed Ronnie off the cliff? Someone like Steve Matlock, avenging his father's death?

'Nice work, mate!' Nick patted Scott on the back as he mastered a series of complicated riffs. ' Sweet sounds! Looks like I've got competition.'

Scott was so confused he thought his brain would implode. This was like one of those exercises they gave you at school on Personal Development days to see if you knew right from wrong: *You get to play guitar with your all-time hero, but you suspect that your hero is a cold-blooded psychopath with the morals of a hungry stoat. Do you a) just have fun and not worry about a few silly old crimes, b) walk away with your conscience intact, or c) sit and squirm?*

Suddenly the guitar strings felt like razor wires under Scott's fingers. 'Cheers, thanks!' he mumbled, thrusting the guitar back into Nick's hands. 'Got to go. Need to, er, take Drift home.'

Stopping only to scoop Drift up in his arms, Scott fled the tent in such a hurry that he ran straight into Flak Petersen.

Fifteen

A Visit to the Grand Vista

Meanwhile Jack and Emily were gazing up at the Grand Vista Hotel in Tregower. The pale stone glowed even through the drizzle, and warm golden light shone from four floors of long, elegant windows, some of which were adorned with small balconies of delicate, iron scroll work or window boxes full of daffodils.

Emily looked over her shoulder at the war memorial. She was right. You'd definitely be able to see the soldier

– complete with seagull perched on his helmet – from those rooms on the second floor. 'Come on,' she called to Jack as she skipped up the flight of broad stone steps and between a pair of fluted stone pillars, and pushed open an imposing door, glistening with deep-red gloss paint. 'Just remember to stick to the plan and we'll be fine.'

The lobby was lit by two enormous chandeliers, the light reflecting off acres of dark wood panelling and gleaming chocolate-brown leather sofas. The air was full of tinkly jazz music and the expensive scents of wax polish and fresh flowers.

'Can I help you?'

The voice came from a gangling young man behind the reception desk. He wore a dark green waistcoat with shiny gold buttons over a white shirt. His name badge gave his name as Omar.

'We've come to meet our uncle.' Emily almost had to stand on tiptoe to see over the desk. 'He's visiting from America.'

'We're a bit early,' Jack added, looking at his watch and reciting the script they'd practised on the way. 'Could you call his room and let him know we're here?'

Omar looked up and flicked hair off his large round glasses – he had the same floppy fringe as Scott, only in a jet-black rather than light brown version. 'What's your uncle's name?'

Emily smiled sweetly. 'Ronnie Brandon.'

Omar tapped on the keyboard of his computer. Then

he shook his head. 'Sorry, there's no one of that name staying here. Are you quite sure you have the right hotel?'

If only you knew! Jack thought. Then suddenly he had an idea. What was that name Ronnie had used to hire the car, his wife's name? 'Try Kojak!'

'Not Kojak, Novak!' Emily corrected, kicking Jack's ankle.

Omar peered out from under his fringe, his eyes flickering with suspicion behind his glasses.

'It's his, er, stage name,' Emily explained.

Omar tapped again and scanned the computer screen. 'Novak. Here we are.' He picked up the phone from the desk in front of him, pressed three keys and held the receiver to his ear. 'No reply!' He glanced back at his screen. 'Actually, we've not seen Mr Novak for a couple of days . . . although his things are still in his room.'

'He keeps himself to himself,' Emily said quickly. 'Like I said, we're early. We'll just wait here for him.'

Pulling Jack with her, Emily darted to the sofa in the farthest corner and slid across the slippery leather. 'Aggh! That's so annoying. He didn't say the room number.'

Jack grinned. 'It's a good thing some of us are trained in the art of detailed observation.' He sat back and folded his arms. Oh, how he loved being able to beat Emily at her own game just once in a while!

'Go on, tell me!' Emily hissed. 'Otherwise I'll be

forced to extract the information using my kick-boxing skills!' She landed a fake karate chop on Jack's arm. An elderly couple sipping tea on the other side of the lobby shot them a disapproving glance.

'OK, I surrender,' Jack laughed. 'It's five one two.'

Emily twitched her eyebrows. 'How do you know?'

Jack just smiled smugly. But only for a moment. This kind of genius had to be shared. 'I could see the computer screen in Omar's glasses.'

Emily could only nod in silent admiration. Then she looked round for the stairs. 'As soon as Omar's not looking, follow me!'

'You must have got it wrong,' Emily groaned. She and Jack had been sneaking round the thickly carpeted corridors of the Grand Vista Hotel for eons. *There was no room five one two.*

Jack shook his head. 'I know it said five one two. The reflection was dead clear.'

Suddenly Emily slapped her forehead and laughed. 'Of course, that's the point! It was a *reflection*! Like mirror writing, the numbers are the wrong way round. It's not five one two, it's two one five!'

'Oh, yeah!' Jack mimed shooting himself. 'Tell you what, let's not tell Scott we wasted twenty minutes looking for the wrong room.'

'Deal,' Emily agreed. 'Come on, we passed two one five. It's on the second floor.'

Jack and Emily were in luck. As they entered the second-floor corridor, a chambermaid approached, pushing a trolley laden with cleaning materials. While Emily lured the maid to the other end of the corridor with a story about looking for a dropped earring, Jack 'borrowed' the master key-card from the trolley, slid it into the lock of room two one five and wedged the door ajar with a wad of paper from Emily's notebook. Then he slipped the key back onto the trolley.

Moments later, they were standing in the middle of room two one five. Tastefully decorated in shades of cream and pale green, it contained the usual hotel furniture of bed, armchair, desk and wardrobe. Jack ran to the tall window with its floor-length brocade curtains, looked out onto the seafront and saluted the World War One soldier marching past on his column. Then, fighting back the urge to jump on the bed and check out the movie channels on the TV, he joined Emily in the search for the tape.

'Look!' Emily cried, spotting a half-open suitcase on a bench by the door. 'Maybe it's in here.' She rummaged through the shirts and jeans and jackets, but there was no sign of a tape. It wasn't in any of the drawers of the bedside table, either, or on the coffee table or in the en suite bathroom, which was as white and sparkling as an ice rink.

Jack was starting to think they were onto a loser, when he caught sight of a fluffy, white dressing gown on a hook on the bathroom door. He couldn't resist trying it on for size and admiring himself in the all-round mirrors.

When he wandered back into the bedroom, he found Emily gazing into the wardrobe. He looked over her shoulder. There was a shirt on a hanger, some spare pillows and a travel iron, otherwise the shelves were empty except for a chunky, grey metal box.

'It's a safe,' Emily said flatly. 'You know, to lock your valuables in.'

'I do know what a safe is,' Jack laughed. 'Most hotel rooms have them.'

'This must be where Ronnie's hidden the tape.'

Jack stared at the numerical keypad on the front of the safe. 'Great!' he sighed. 'If we knew the combination we'd be laughing.'

That's when he heard the voices outside the door and the little click of a card key-card being inserted into the lock.

Sixteen

The Holy Grail

Emily and Jack grabbed each other by both arms, as if about to dance a tango, and stared at each other, eyes wide as satellite dishes.

Without saying a word, they dived under the bed.

Emily peeled a discarded sock from her forehead. Yuk! It was dark and dusty under here, but at least they were hidden by the thick, floor-length bedspread.

Deafened by her heart pounding like one of Ronnie's

drum solos, Emily could barely hear anything at first. As her heartbeat calmed down she could make out a woman talking. Had one of the chambermaids come to clean the room? Was she talking to herself? Perhaps they worked in pairs? Emily lifted her nose a few millimetres from the carpet and peeped out from under the bedspread.

What she saw gave her such a shock she almost shrieked out loud. The woman had her back to the bed and was wearing plain black leggings and a white shirt, but there was no mistaking her petite figure and short, expensively cut hair the colour of cherry juice.

It was Lauren Wade!

But of course, Emily thought. *It makes sense. Lauren is Nick Dylan's girlfriend. He must have told her all about the scheme to silence Ronnie, and now she's helping him by looking for the tape – just like she helps him by taking the chillies out of his curry and making sure nobody disturbs him when he's meditating!*

Suddenly Emily heard a second voice, a man's this time. 'Nick Dylan's here too!' she murmured under her breath.

Nice one, Scotto! Jack fumed as he wriggled forward to peep out next to Emily. *You're meant to be tailing Nick and you've only let the guy follow us to the hotel, stroll into our operation and snarf the vital tape right under our noses! Brilliant work!*

But then he heard a volley of swearing so extreme his

ears blushed. There was only one man Jack knew who had such a jaw-dropping vocabulary of rude words, some of which he'd never heard before, even outside the kebab shop on a Saturday night. It was Billy Riordan!

What was Billy Riordan doing in Ronnie's hotel room with Lauren? For one revolting moment, Jack thought they must be having a love affair behind Nick Dylan's back. If this turned out to be some soppy snog-fest, he would literally die of embarrassment only to be found by a cleaner, weeks later, a skeleton under the bed along with that old sock.

But when he could finally bring himself to look again, Jack saw this was clearly no romantic liaison. Lauren and Billy were ripping the room apart! It seemed they were looking for the tape too. It was like the Holy Grail or the crystal skull in one of those Indiana Jones films.

'Where the *beepety-beep* has the *beeping beeper* put the *beeping* thing?' Billy roared, his long black hair flying around his head.

'How should I know!' Lauren snapped.

'Beep,' Billy spat, yanking open the wardrobe door, 'there's a safe!'

Lauren hurried to his side. 'We'll need the combination.'

'Don't touch the keypad!' Billy yelled. 'These things only give you three attempts to get it right before the alarm goes off.'

'OK,' Lauren said. 'Here's what we'll do. We've got

Ronnie's key-card and his ID from his wallet. You just go down to reception, pretend to be Ronnie and say you've forgotten the combination. Then ask them to come and reset the safe for you.'

Billy made a kind of growling noise. 'Won't they notice I'm not Ronnie? I don't look much like his photo on this ID card.' He ran his hand over his hair, and gestured at his studded leather jacket and ripped jeans.

Lauren laughed. 'I'll come with you and flirt with that dopey young guy on reception. That should distract him from staring at the photo.' She undid the top few buttons of her blouse and wiggled towards the door.

'Come on,' Emily hissed, as soon as the door shut behind Billy and Lauren. 'There's no time to lose! We've got to get that tape out before they get back.'

'How?' Jack asked, squeezing out from under the bed and shedding the dressing gown like a snake skin. 'We haven't got the combination either.'

'I know!' Emily was standing by the wardrobe, bobbing up and down with a tortured expression on her face. 'Think!' she howled, more to herself than to Jack. '*Think!* What numbers would Ronnie have used for his safe combination?'

'What about his date of birth or something?' Jack suggested.

'Wouldn't that be too obvious?'

'You sound like Scott,' Jack complained. 'He's always

ranting about how dim people are when it comes to choosing passwords and PIN numbers, always picking something like their cat's name or their kid's birthday when they should select random numbers . . .'

Emily ground her teeth. 'If it's random we've got no chance, but we've got to try something!'

Jack shrugged. 'Well, Ronnie isn't a computer freak like Scott. He's just your simple rock 'n' roll cowboy drummer. Maybe he *did* go for the obvious.'

'OK, but what could it be? Kids? Pets?' Suddenly Emily clapped her hands. 'What about Rosa? His wife! Ronnie has her name tattooed on his arm. Maybe he uses her birthday as his number . . .'

'Oh, yeah, we're on fire!' Jack's hand was already poised for a celebratory high-five when he realized the fatal flaw in their brilliance. He slapped the wall in frustration instead. 'Minor problem – we don't know Rosa's birthday.'

But Emily was grinning. 'That's where you're wrong!' She rummaged in her bag, grabbed her notebook and shook out the print-outs from Scott's internet research. 'I know it's here, somewhere,' she murmured, dropping to her knees to rifle through the scattered pages. 'It's in that bit about Ronnie marrying Rosa. It had their ages and everything. Here it is!' She waved a sheet of paper in triumph. 'Rosa Marie Novak, born sixth February 1951. February is the second month, so that would make the four-number combination six, two, five, one.'

Jack reached for the keypad on the safe, his hand trembling.

'Quick!' Emily hissed. 'They'll be back any second!'

Jack jabbed at the keys: six, two, five, one. Then he waited. Nothing happened. He tugged at the handle. Nothing happened. At last, a message came up on the display: *Incorrect.*

'Incorrect?' Jack shouted at the safe. 'What do you mean *incorrect*? Come on! Work with me! This is an emergency!'

'Try just the date and month,' Emily suggested. 'Zero, six, zero, two.'

'You do it! You might have more luck.'

Emily took a deep breath and entered the numbers with a quivering finger.

Incorrect!

Emily clutched at her hair and stared at Jack. 'Oh, no! Only one chance left.' This was a nightmare. They were so close and yet so far away. She was sure the tape was behind that metal door. All that stood in their way was four piddling little numbers!

Jack felt the same. After all their work getting into the room and the total genius of his reflected-room-number brainwave, how could they fall at the last hurdle? Suddenly a tiny germ of an idea began to sprout in his brain. He couldn't quite put his finger on it at first . . . something to do with reflected numbers, numbers the wrong way round . . . back to front . . . 'I've got it!'

he blurted. 'Ronnie's American! They do their dates the other way round, don't they? The month first, then the date.'

'Of course!' Emily exclaimed. 'It's not six, two, five, one. It's two, six, five, one.'

Jack grinned. 'Go for it!'

Emily shook her head. 'You. I'm shaking too much.'

Jack heard footsteps and voices in the corridor outside. It was now or never. Before he could chicken out, he jabbed at the keys: two, six, five, one.

He could hardly bear to look at the display. He heard a click as someone slid the key-card into the door. His heart plummeted. Then he heard another click. He opened his eyes. The word *Open* was flashing on the safe's display. In a single move, Emily had pulled open the safe door, reached inside, grabbed a brown padded envelope and stuffed it into her bag. The door to the room was opening now. It was too late to make it back under the bed. Instead, Jack pulled Emily to the long window on the back wall.

They flung themselves behind the green brocade curtains.

Just in time.

Emily heard Lauren giggle. 'Sorry to drag you up here, Omar, but I popped all my jewellery inside and forgot my number. Head like a sieve!'

There was a moment's silence. Then Omar's puzzled voice. 'But this safe is already open, madam.'

'Goodness, is it really?' Lauren gasped. 'I was *sure* it was locked.'

Billy swore.

'Your nephew and niece are waiting down in the lobby, by the way,' Omar said politely on his way out.

'What are you on about, man?' Billy yelled after him. Then he swore some more. He thundered around the room like a rhino gone berserk, snatching things up and crashing them down. 'That safe was locked when we left this room!' he raged. 'Someone's been in here and pinched that tape!'

'Calm down, Billy,' Lauren pleaded as a bedside lamp smashed against the wall.

'It's those kids, isn't it?' Billy roared. 'You said they were asking Ronnie about the tape in the hospital.'

Emily couldn't believe her ears. Lauren had heard them talking to Ronnie. *But how?* Then suddenly it all fell into place. That social worker who was talking to Harry Stiles! Emily could have punched herself on the nose. She'd been fooled by a wig, a pair of unfashionable shoes, a fake ID card and a clipboard! *A clipboard, for goodness' sake! The oldest trick in the book! OK, so Lauren has the advantage of being a professional actress, but I should have seen straight through that pathetic disguise!*

'But Emily and the boys *can't* have known Ronnie was staying in this room,' Lauren told Billy. 'He couldn't even remember the name of the hotel! The only reason we knew was because we found his room keys in his wallet . . .'

Emily pricked up her ears. *Lauren had Ronnie's wallet.* Did that mean Nick had stolen it when he met Ronnie at West Rock Beach? But before she could puzzle it over any further, she had a more immediate problem to solve.

Billy Riordan was still storming around the room like a tornado. 'Just wait till I catch them. I'll strangle them with my bare hands!' Now he was millimetres away from the window. The thick curtain fabric trembled as he brushed against it, then twitched as a hand reached out and grasped where the edges met.

Emily closed her eyes and held her breath. Any second, the curtains would be swept back and . . .

'Stop going on about those stupid kids!' Lauren snapped. 'Even if they did find this room, how would they know the combination to open the safe? No one's been in here. The safe must have just been jammed or something. And the tape's not there anyway! Come on, let's get out of here!'

Billy moved away from the window.

Phew! At last, Emily could breathe again.

'Hang on. What's this poking out from under the bed?' Billy said suddenly. 'This dressing gown wasn't here before. I was right. Those kids *have* been in here! And I bet they're still hiding!'

Jack felt his stomach turn to water. How could he have

been so dumb as to leave the dressing gown behind? He heard Billy drag the bed away from the wall. 'Not here.'

'They're not in the bathroom either!' Lauren shouted.

Jack heard Billy open the wardrobe door and knew it could only be a matter of moments before he looked behind the curtains. There just weren't that many hiding places in a medium-sized hotel room.

There was only one thing for it!

Seventeen

Disappeared!

'Are you mad?' Emily hissed. 'We're two floors up!'

But Jack continued opening the window – easing it as gently as he could to avoid making a noise. 'We'll be fine,' he whispered urgently. 'I'm sure this room has a balcony. From there, we can drop down to the one below.'

The gap was big enough to squeeze through now. Jack leaned out.

There was no balcony.

But there was no turning back either. With the words *strangle them with my bare hands* ringing in his ears, Jack climbed out on to the narrowest of ledges, holding out his hand to guide Emily out after him. He shuffled sideways, away from the window, whispering for Emily to do the same in the other direction.

There were only two thoughts in Emily's head as she pressed her back against the stonework and inched along the ledge. The first was, *Thank goodness Drift is safe with Scott.* The second was, *What was I thinking, following Jack out of a second-floor window?*

'Just hang on and don't look down!' Jack whispered.

Emily hadn't any intention of looking down, but as soon as she heard Jack's words, she couldn't stop herself. Beneath her, the porch over the hotel's front entrance, the stone steps and the pavement swayed and swam as if under water. She'd never been scared of heights before, but then she'd never balanced two floors up, on the outside of a hotel wall, on a ledge no wider than a skirting board before either. She closed her eyes and felt her knees turn to porridge.

'Grab onto that flagpole just above your head!' Jack hissed.

Slowly Emily slid her hand up over the stonework until she felt the cold, solid metal. As she locked her fingers round the pole, a third thought entered her head: *If I ever get out of this, I'm going to kill Jack Carter!*

At that moment she heard Billy roar.

'*Beeeeeeeep!* The little devils have scarpered through the window. They must have had ropes or something.'

Emily flattened herself against the wall, willing her body to melt into the stone. Out of the corner of her eye, she could see Billy's long black hair and the tip of his nose sticking out through the open window. Surely, any second now he'd lean out further and see them clinging there like a pair of moths. He must be able to feel the window frame shaking from the trembling of her knees.

But Billy Riordan just slapped his palms on the glass and roared, 'They'll be on the way to the hospital now to give that tape to Ronnie. Come on! I'm going to shut Ronnie up once and for all, whatever it takes. And if I see those kids . . .'

A moment later Jack heard the door of the hotel room slam. Billy and Lauren had gone. He climbed back in through the window and helped Emily to crawl in after him.

'Woohoo!' he whooped, jumping up and down on the bed and punching the air. 'That was a close one! Was that awesome or was that *awesome*? I'm so stoked! It's better than when I did that bungee jump at—'

Jack suddenly noticed that Emily wasn't joining the celebrations. In fact, she was marching towards the door in silence. But then she spun round and leaped across the room towards him.

Jack stalled, wobbling slightly on the springy mattress. For a moment he thought Emily was going to fell him with one of her kick-boxing moves. But instead – unable to keep her excitement from bubbling over – she jumped up and joined him in a wild victory bounce. 'We did it!' she laughed. 'We got the tape and we escaped from Billy Riordan!' She pulled the brown envelope from her bag and waved it around her head. 'We were like Spider-Man out there!'

Suddenly they heard banging on the wall behind them. 'Keep the noise down!' someone shouted from the next room.

Giggling, the two friends clapped their hands over their mouths and stopped bouncing.

'For a minute there,' Jack panted, as they headed for the door, 'I thought you were really mad at me for leaving that dressing gown on the floor and then leading you out onto the ledge!'

Emily poked her head out to check the corridor was clear. She turned to Jack. 'I was! I was planning to kill you,' she whispered seriously. 'But it'll have to wait,' she added with a grin. ' Right now, we've got work to do. We've got to stop those two getting to Ronnie.'

~

As they unlocked their bikes from a palm tree on the seafront, Jack looked up and noticed Omar hurrying down the steps of the hotel, steered at the elbow by a very flustered elderly lady.

'There are kids up there, climbing around on the

walls like little monkeys!' she insisted. 'It shouldn't be allowed.' She pointed up at a second-floor window above the front door. 'Right there!'

Omar looked up. 'I can't see anything,' he said. 'Except that the flagpole looks a bit crooked.'

The old lady shook her head. 'I know what I saw, young man! What are you going to do about it?'

Omar shrugged in bewilderment.

What with magically opening safes, disappearing nephews and nieces, and old ladies hallucinating about children climbing on the walls, it had been a funny sort of day at the Grand Vista Hotel.

Meanwhile, Scott had given up stalking Nick Dylan – who had gone back to his knitting and was still refusing to act in a suspicious manner. He'd tried phoning Emily and Jack to see how the hotel mission was going, but both had had their phones switched off for ages. Unsure what to do next, Scott carefully installed Drift in the bike basket again and headed for the hollow tree HQ to await further communications. He took Drift to the stream for a drink of water, then climbed up to the observation branch among the rustling leaves, while Drift ran around chasing squirrels. He was watching the traffic buzz across the causeway through the binoculars, when he caught sight of a car he recognized. He'd admired the vintage white sports car at the end of

Castle Key harbour, where the guests at The Lighthouse parked their cars. It belonged to Lauren Wade.

Scott adjusted the focus on the binoculars. Yes, it was definitely Lauren. The sunroof was down and he could see her bright red hair. *Weird,* he thought. Nick said Lauren had been shopping in Carrickstowe all day. So how come she was heading north across the causeway from Castle Key to the mainland now? And wasn't that Billy Riordan in the passenger seat? And why were they driving at about a hundred miles an hour?

Scott didn't know the answers, but the hairs rising on the back of his neck told him they might just involve Ronnie Brandon.

'Come on, Drift!' he called. 'We've got to get to the hospital.'

Drift's ears drooped momentarily. He'd started to recognize the word *hospital* and he'd added it to his blacklist of Bad Places – along with *vet* and *school.* He knew it would mean sitting outside on Lookout Duty again! But he wagged his tail dutifully and hopped into the basket. Emily had entrusted him with the top-priority mission of looking after Scott for the afternoon, and he certainly wasn't going to let her down.

~

Scott raced through the hospital, his sense of unease growing all the time, like a balloon inflating in his chest. When he reached Ronnie's ward, he peeped through the window in the door. It wasn't visiting time but luckily the coast was clear; Nurse Redpath was busy teaching a group of junior nurses a new procedure. Scott slipped in and crept along the ward.

A green curtain had been pulled around Ronnie's bed. Assuming that Dr Obi must be with him, Scott waited outside, not wanting to intrude. Seconds passed. And then minutes. There was no hint of movement from behind the curtain, no whisper of a sound. *What are they doing in there?* he wondered.

Praying he wasn't about to witness some kind of embarrassing private examination, Scott tweaked back the curtain and peeped through the gap.

There was nobody there!

Scott did a double take.

The drum kit was still there. The bunch of daffodils Emily had brought in was still there. Today's copy of *The Carrickstowe Times* was still there.

But Ronnie Brandon had disappeared.

Scott backed away from the curtain, dread settling over him like a thick woollen blanket. He tried to shake it off. *Ronnie's probably just gone for some X-rays or physio or something*, he told himself. With a glance along the ward to make sure Nurse Redpath was still occupied, he hurried to Harry Stiles's bedside.

The old man looked up from his crossword puzzle. 'You back again? Can't keep away from the place, eh?'

'Did you see where Ronnie went?' Scott asked.

'A nurse came and took him off for some brain scans a few minutes ago. Pretty little thing: curly blonde hair, Welsh accent . . .'

But Scott wasn't listening. He was already in the corridor, looking for signs to the brain scan department.

It's probably fine, he kept repeating to himself. After all, Dr Obi *said* that Ronnie would be having brain scans to help find out about his memory loss. There was nothing to worry about. He'd just go and check that Ronnie was OK and then try to track down Emily and Jack – who *still* hadn't switched their phones on.

He passed the ICU, the ENT department and A&E, then stopped to ask for directions.

'Brain scan department?' a helpful nurse repeated. 'I think you mean Radiography. Turn right and take the stairs to the basement.'

Scott ran all the way until he came to a door covered with signs and arrows: X-ray, CT, MRI. What was it with hospitals and calling things by their initials? He was about to enter when he caught sight of Dr Obi hurrying around a bend in the corridor carrying a pile of charts.

Scott chased after him. 'I need to talk to Ronnie,' he panted when he caught up. 'Do you know how long his brain scans will take?'

Dr Obi blinked in surprise. 'Brain scans? You must be mistaken. I've not ordered any scans for Ronnie today.'

Eighteen

V. V. Dangerous

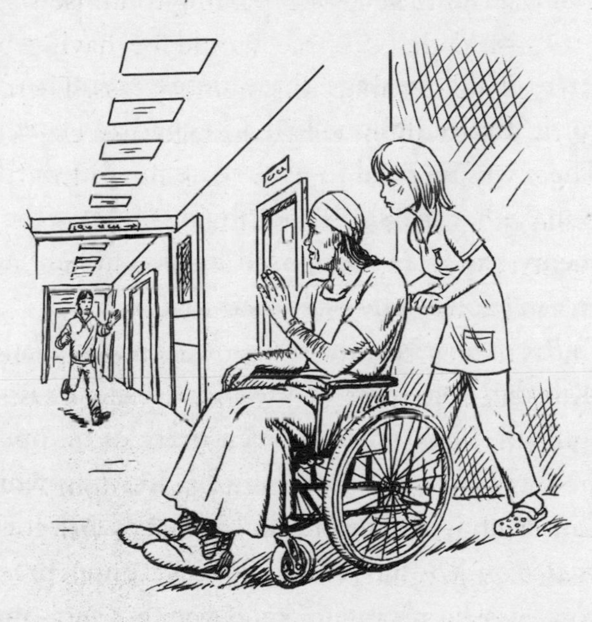

Dr Obi shook his head. He looked wearier than ever. 'A nurse took Ronnie for scans? That can't be right. Ronnie had his CT and MRI scans last night. Any nurse would've seen that from his chart.'

Scott felt the blanket of dread tighten around him, squeezing the air out of his lungs. When his phone rang in his pocket he almost jumped out of his skin.

Dr Obi raised his eyebrows. 'You do know phones should be switched off in the hospital.'

'Sorry, I forgot,' Scott murmured, as he glanced down at the text message.

LW+BR in on it. V.v. dangerous. Keep watch on RB. On way.

Scott read the message three times, trying to make sense of it. Emily's phone had a keypad and predictive text. There was no need to use shortcuts. But she didn't like to make her messages too obvious in case they fell into enemy hands. He supposed he should be thankful it wasn't in Morse code or something!

LW+BR in on it? Emily must mean Lauren Wade and Billy Riordan were part of the plot to silence Ronnie. Scott gulped. Nick must be even more of an operator than he'd thought, calmly doing his knitting while he sent Lauren and Billy out to do his dirty work for him! *Keep watch on RB?* RB was obviously Ronnie Brandon. But how was he meant to keep watch over someone who'd already disappeared? *V.v. dangerous . . .*

With stomach-clenching certainty, Scott suddenly knew what had happened. That pretty blonde nurse Harry had seen taking Ronnie away? That was no nurse. *It was Lauren Wade in disguise.* And Scott had a feeling that whatever Lauren and Billy had planned for Ronnie's brain, it didn't involve scanning machines.

Blunt objects were more likely to be on the agenda.

Scott knew he had to do something, and fast. 'Ronnie Brandon's in danger,' he told Dr Obi urgently. 'We have to find him.'

The doctor hesitated. 'Well, he could have just gone for a walk . . .'

'NO!' Scott yelled. He fought to get his voice back under control. 'You said yourself that a *real* nurse would know Ronnie had already had his scans.'

Dr Obi massaged his bloodshot eyes with his palms. 'Well, that's true. And the police did say we needed to keep an eye out for anyone suspicious looking for Ronnie . . . Alright, I'll get onto security.' He picked up the receiver of an emergency phone on the wall and shouted instructions. 'I've asked for a Code Nine,' he explained to Scott. 'It stops anyone leaving the hospital. It's usually used if someone tries to take a baby or a child without permission.'

Shouting his thanks to Dr Obi over his shoulder, Scott ran back towards the main entrance, but when he reached the big double doors there was no sign of Lauren and Ronnie. Was he too late? If Lauren had already managed to get Ronnie out of the hospital to her car – where, no doubt, Billy Riordan was waiting – he'd probably never be seen or heard of again.

Scott scanned the concourse. Security guards were already pacing around, muttering into their walkie-talkies and explaining to groups of irritated people that they were not allowed to exit due to a 'security incident'. *Of course,* he thought, *Lauren wouldn't leave this way anyway. The main doors would always be the most heavily patrolled . . .*

Scott had spent so much time hanging around the hospital lately he had a good idea where all the entrances, fire exits and delivery bays were located. He checked them all. As he sprinted from one to the next he tried to figure out how Lauren was planning to get Ronnie to leave with her. Had she tricked him into co-operating by saying he had to have another type of scan – in another building perhaps? Or could she simply have drugged him? In a hospital, nobody would take much notice of a nurse pushing an unconscious man along in a wheelchair.

Scott kept running through the labyrinth of corridors, past signs that said *No Public Access,* venturing into remote underground regions of the hospital. He was completely lost now, and giving up all hope of ever finding Ronnie, when a blonde nurse pushing a man in a wheelchair appeared round a corner and almost ran into him.

Ronnie – who was wearing nothing but his hospital gown and a blanket over his legs – looked up and waved. 'Hey, there, Scott, what are you doing down here?'

'Oh, I just got a bit lost,' Scott mumbled, playing for time. 'Er, how about you?'

'I'm supposed to be going for a brain scan in some other hospital,' Ronnie said. 'But there's a big security alert going on, so we're having to go out the back way.' He smiled up at the nurse. 'Nurse Swinton is taking good care of me! It's nice not being bossed around by the lovely Redpath for a change.'

Nurse Swinton smiled. Her blonde hair curled around her face, her cheeks were plump and her eyes were a vibrant peacock-feather blue. *Amazing what you can do with a good wig, a bit of padding and some coloured contact lenses,* Scott thought. Above the smile, the nurse regarded him with a cool, hard stare. But Scott detected the flicker of recognition she was trying to hide.

She knows who I am, Scott thought. *But, more importantly, does she know that I know who* she *is?*

'Well, we must press on. Ronnie here needs that scan urgently.' Nurse Swinton spoke with a strong Welsh accent, and attempted a jolly no-nonsense manner, but her voice was brittle with tension. She gave the wheelchair a shove and began to move off along the corridor, so fast the wheels screeched on the scuffed beige tiles.

'Here, let me help you,' Scott offered, beetling to her side.

Nurse Swinton yanked the handles out of Scott's reach. 'Hospital policy. Only qualified nursing staff are allowed to operate the wheelchairs.'

Right! And you'd know all about being qualified nursing staff, wouldn't you, Lauren? Scott seethed. But he forced a smile. 'OK. I'll just tag along with you guys until we find a way out of this place.'

As they trundled along the corridor, Scott felt his spirits rise. He'd beaten the time bomb and found Ronnie. All he had to do was stick to him like superglue. Sooner or later they'd come across a security guard and then he could raise the alarm. If the worst came to the worst, he could overpower Lauren anyway.

Lauren was clearly thinking along the same lines. Her lips were pressed together so tightly they were turning white and her eyes flicked from side to side, searching for a way out.

Scott allowed himself a quiet moment of gloating. *Scott Carter: one. Bad Guys: nil.* He couldn't wait to tell Emily and Jack how he'd tracked Lauren Wade down and then single-handedly orchestrated her capture.

But it seemed his gloating had come just a little too soon.

'*Beeeeeeeeeep!*' The hurricane-force swear word came blasting down the corridor, followed by the lumbering bulk of Billy Riordan. 'What the *beeping beep* is keeping you?' he bellowed at Lauren. 'I've been growing old waiting for you to bring him out.'

'They've locked the place down, if you hadn't noticed!' Lauren snapped.

Suddenly Billy noticed Scott. 'I know you! You're one of those blasted rug-rats from The Lighthouse! I know you lot nicked the tape from the safe and then climbed out of the window with a rope! So where's the tape?'

Scott's head whirled with so many thoughts it was making him dizzy. Jack and Emily must have got the tape from the hotel before Billy found it. *Climbed out through the window with a rope?* Scott dreaded to think what kind of stunt Jack and Emily had pulled! At least Billy hadn't caught them, but where were they now?

'Like I'm going to tell you!' Scott said, hoping he sounded a lot braver than he felt.

But before Billy could reply, a voice piped up from the wheelchair. 'You're Billy Riordan, aren't you? What are you doing here?' Ronnie rubbed his eyes as if trying to adjust the focus. 'What did you mean *bring him out*? You don't work for the hospital, do you?'

'That's enough questions!' Billy smashed his fist against the wall. 'Where's the tape?'

Ronnie stared up at him. 'I don't remember.'

'Don't come the innocent with me!' Beneath his long black hair, Billy Riordan's cavernous face was turning a dangerous shade of crimson. He hoisted Ronnie up by the scruff of his hospital gown until they were eyeball to eyeball. 'You'll tell me where that tape is, or else!' Billy screamed. Then he let Ronnie fall back into the wheelchair.

Scott scanned the long corridor with its walls the exact shade of mushy peas. It was deserted. *How are we going to get out of this alive?* But before Scott had time to think of an answer, Ronnie suddenly lunged at Billy's legs. Caught off guard, Billy stumbled backwards. Scott helped him on his way with a well-placed kick to the back of his knees.

Billy hit the ground like a falling oak tree as Ronnie staggered to his feet.

Scott saw his chance. He grabbed hold of the wheelchair and slammed it into Billy, knocking him down as he tried to get up.

'Run!' Ronnie yelled.

Scott didn't need to be told twice. He dashed away down the corridor. Looking back over his shoulder, he saw Billy Riordan roaring and cursing as he got to his feet. Lauren was trying to push the wheelchair out of his path.

Scott had expected Ronnie to be right behind him. He was the one who'd shouted 'Run!', after all!

That's when Scott realized that Ronnie hadn't thought through his escape strategy very well. In fact, he hadn't thought it through *at all.* Outrunning your attackers relies on one very simple principle: being able to *run*!

But Ronnie was now tottering along with all the speed of an arthritic snail, the hospital gown flapping around his bare white legs.

Billy would catch up with him any second.

Nineteen

Right Out of Options

Scott stared back down the corridor, his heart sinking so fast it was tunnelling to Australia.

Instinctively, his hand flew to his cheek. The scar from the jagged rock in Keyhole Cove was itching, as if to remind him that he'd risked his life once already to rescue Ronnie Brandon; he wasn't going to let Billy Riordan get his hands on him now. Without another thought, Scott ripped a fire extinguisher from the wall, pulled out the pin and charged at Billy, spraying the jet of foam at his face. Billy slapped his hands over his eyes but it was too late. He lurched from side to side, screaming oaths and curses.

'Come on!' Scott grabbed Ronnie by the arm and half dragged, half carried him along the corridor. 'Let's get out of here.'

Scott knew his fire extinguisher attack could only provide a temporary reprieve. Billy would soon recover his senses and come after them – madder than ever. Given their serious handicap in the moving-at-speed department, their only chance was to hide.

'Through here,' Scott urged, throwing open the first door he came to. They hobbled into a laboratory, past rows of microscopes, racks of blood samples in test tubes, and wall charts illustrating hideous disease processes. A second door led into a deserted workshop full of vices and grinders and cutting machines. Scott pulled Ronnie along between the benches, searching for somewhere to hide. Suddenly he felt something brush against his leg. He looked down to see a pallid white hand reaching out from a half-open drawer. He jumped away in horror and backed into a dangling skeleton, which clattered to the ground in a heap of bones. Scott whipped round to see a pair of disembodied feet marching along a shelf. *What was this place?*

'Artificial limbs!' Ronnie panted. 'Must be where they make them.'

'Yeah, I knew that!' Scott said weakly, dragging Ronnie to another door. There could be a secret portal to another universe in here for all he knew, but he wasn't hanging around to find out! The workshop was freaking him out. And, anyway, Billy was already behind them, firing curses like bullets. They stumbled out into another corridor, staggered down a ramp and dived through a swing door.

A steamy, soapy wave of heat rolled over them. Everywhere Scott looked, industrial-sized washing machines and tumble dryers were swooshing and gurgling and rumbling. It was like entering the bowels of a giant beast.

'This way!' Scott tugged Ronnie towards a row of enormous carts at the back of the laundry. The carts – huge wire cages on wheels – were stacked with piles of neatly folded white sheets. 'In here!' He pushed Ronnie onto a cart that had one of its sides propped open. Clutching his broken ribs and gasping with pain, Ronnie burrowed under the sheets.

At least it's clean laundry, Scott thought as he crawled in behind Ronnie and pulled the starched bedding over their heads.

Just in time. Billy Riordan's X-rated thundering could be heard over the thrum of the machines.

'*Beep!* I know you're in here!' he roared. 'You can't hide forever!'

Quaking with fear, Scott peeked out through a gap

in the sheets. Billy Riordan was stampeding around the laundry, wielding a length of thick metal pipe in both hands and smashing it down on everything in his path like a giant battle-axe. *Crash, clang, bang.* He was coming closer and closer, bouncing the pipe off the metal rails and struts of the carts and thwacking it down on the piles of laundry. Scott braced himself for impact . . .

'Agggh!' Ronnie shrieked. Four folded sheets weren't much to soften the blow of an iron bar on a broken rib.

'Ha!' Billy laughed wildly. 'What have we here?' He began to pull away the sheets, while continuing to hammer with the pipe, as if he were playing Splat the Rat.

'Agggh!' Scott tried to bite back the cry as the pipe hit his shoulder. The pain that jolted through him was like a million stubbed toes all at once. Another blow glanced off his cheek, knocking the scab off his scar. Behind him, Ronnie groaned as the next blow landed on his knee.

Scott knew they had to give themselves up before they were mashed to a pulp. He sat up with his hands over his head. 'OK, OK!' he yelled. 'I surrender!'

Ronnie did the same.

'Ha! Flushed out like vermin!' Billy roared in triumph, slamming the cart shut with a clang that echoed round the laundry. He squinted at Ronnie, his pale blue eyes spidered with red veins from the fire extinguisher foam. 'We're going to end this now. Where's the tape?'

But Ronnie was gazing past Billy with the same distant look in his eyes as when he first started to regain his memory. He pointed a quivering finger at the woman who'd followed Billy into the room. Her blonde wig had come askew in the chase to reveal the short red hair beneath, and she'd lost the padding from her cheeks.

'I know you!' Ronnie stated in a zombie-like tone. 'You're not a nurse. It's coming back to me now. I was meant to meet Nick at West Rock Beach, but Nick didn't come. You turned up instead – and you offered me money to keep quiet—'

'That's enough of this heart-warming reunion!' Billy sneered.

Ronnie's accusing finger swung round to point at Billy. 'And you were there, too! You pushed me off the cliff. *You tried to kill me!*'

'No!' Lauren shouted. 'Billy was just trying to get you to hand over your backpack. We thought you had the tape in there! You lost your grip on the strap and stumbled backwards. It was an accident!'

'You didn't exactly work up a sweat trying to save me though, did you?' Ronnie threw back. 'Look after number one, eh, Billy? Just like after the crash!'

Billy shrugged. 'You hit the rocks. We thought you were dead.'

'How convenient,' Ronnie laughed bitterly. 'The dead can't talk! Like poor Chris Castelli!'

Scott realized that his best chance of getting out of

the laundry cart in one piece, rather than smeared over the end of the iron pipe, was to keep Lauren and Billy talking as long as possible in the hope that someone would come looking for them before Billy flipped his lid again.

'I don't understand. How come *you* guys met Ronnie, instead of Nick?' he asked.

Lauren smiled. 'I *always* check the incoming email on Nick's computer to make sure there's nothing that might upset him. When I saw the blackmail message from Ronnie here—'

'It wasn't blackmail,' Ronnie objected. 'I was giving Nick the chance to do the right thing and clear Chris Castelli's name! I wasn't asking for a penny.'

'Oh, sure! Everyone has their price!' Lauren snapped. 'I didn't even know about the accident – it was way before my time – but I couldn't allow anything to affect Nick's focus for the reunion gig. He's very sensitive to negative energy. So I asked Billy whether it was true that they'd lied about Nick driving . . .'

'Chris was dead,' Billy growled. 'If the press found out Nick was drink-driving, the band would have been finished. There was no point ruining all our careers over a stupid mistake!'

'A *mistake* that killed Chris Castelli and two people in the other car!' Ronnie shouted. 'And ruined the lives of Chris's family. His son Steve is in prison because of what you did!'

'What's the point of dredging up the past?' Billy yelled.

'So you replied from Nick's computer to make Ronnie think it was Nick?' Scott prompted quickly, noticing that Billy was hefting the pipe in his hands, ready to strike again.

Lauren nodded. 'We decided to keep Nick out of it and deal with the situation ourselves.'

That explains why Nick was acting so cool, Scott thought. He wasn't Dr Evil; he was just clueless about the whole thing. But there was still the mystery of why Nick Dylan hadn't recognized the photo of Ronnie on Emily's phone. Suddenly Scott figured it out. *Lauren* was the one who'd shown Nick the picture. But, of course, she hadn't shown him the photo of Ronnie at all, she'd only *pretended* to . . .

Billy banged the pipe on the side of the cart. 'Why couldn't you just give us the tape, take the money and crawl back under your stone? Now, let's stop playing games. Where's the tape? Tell me, or I'll beat it out of you! *Both* of you!'

Scott knew he and Ronnie were right out of options. He couldn't believe his life was going to end like this – cornered in a cage of laundry by a deranged rock star – all because of something that had happened before he was even born! The only good part was that Jack and Emily were safe. The security guards must have stopped them coming into the hospital. But there was so much he still wanted to do: headline with his band at Glastonbury, play Right Back for Chelsea, wake up tomorrow morning . . .

Scott's eyes tracked the pipe as Billy raised it above his head.

Twenty

Sheets, Soap and Surprises

It was all over.

But then, suddenly, Scott's luck changed. The laundry door flew open. Someone had come to rescue them, just in the nick of time! Security guards, police, maybe even a squad of trained marksmen . . .

Oh, no! Scott stared in dismay at the scene unfolding before his eyes. No guards, no police, no marksmen. Just his brother. Charging across the room, emitting a blood-curdling Ninja shriek, and brandishing. . . a sheet!

Scott looked again. Yes, Jack really was about to assault an enraged, pipe-wielding ogre armed only with an item of bed linen. It wasn't even a *double* sheet!

Scott watched as the sheet fluttered down and settled on Billy's head like a wedding veil. Billy shook the sheet off, scooped Jack up and hurled him into the laundry cage, where he landed on top of Scott.

'A sheet?' Scott hissed. 'Couldn't you have found something just a tiny bit more lethal?'

'It was the only thing I could lay my hands on!' Jack protested. 'I didn't know you were in here until I opened the door.'

'Where's that tape?' Billy roared at Jack.

Jack shrugged. 'I haven't got it.'

'So who has? Is it the girl? Where is she?' Billy Riordan raised his arm to aim a blow at Jack's head.

'I'm here!'

Billy whipped round but Emily was already spinning through the air, her leg outstretched, her foot homing in on his wrist. *Thwack!* Right on target! The metal pipe flew out of Billy's hand and soared in a high arc, smashing a light bulb and clattering to the ground in a shower of broken glass. Billy reached down to retrieve his weapon, but before he could make a grab for it, Drift shot out from behind Emily, clamped his teeth round the pipe and dragged it away.

Billy Riordan swore and swiped at Drift, but he missed. He doubled over and pulled a shard of glass from his finger, sucking at the wound to stem the blood.

Scott looked at Jack. 'Quick, now's our chance, before he gets the pipe back!'

Jack nodded and began to climb up the inside of the cage. When he reached the top, Scott passed him a pile of sheets and scrambled up next to him. Each clutching a thick wad of folded sheets to their chests as part shield, part airbag, they launched themselves off the side of the cart.

'Billy, look out!' Lauren gasped.

Billy looked up from his wounded finger, but it was too late. The boys crashed into him, knocking him off balance. The huge man toppled like a skittle. Jack knelt on his back, while Scott pinned his head down with the pile of sheets, muffling the torrent of curses.

'Way to go!' Ronnie Brandon cheered, as he tried, very shakily, to climb out of the cart. 'You brought him down like a rogue steer at a rodeo. If I ever need a couple of new hands on my ranch, I'll know where to look . . .'

Jack grinned, even though the studs on Billy's leather jacket were digging into his knees. One minute he was about to be battered to a purée, the next he was being offered a job as a cowboy. Things were definitely looking up! But his daydreams of life on a Texan ranch were suddenly interrupted. Lauren Wade was making a beeline for Emily's satchel, which was lying near the door where she'd dropped it when she kick-boxed her way into the laundry.

Emily dashed back to intercept her, but Lauren had already seized the bag. She tore open the zips and buckles, turned it upside-down and shook it like a terrier worrying its prey. Notebooks, binoculars, evidence bags, a fire-lighting kit, screwdrivers, a spool of wire, batteries, bandages, a clipboard, a torch, a compass, a phone, a listening device, a magnifying glass, a fingerprint kit and a hundred other items spilled across the laundry floor. Lauren stared for a moment, stunned by the sheer quantity of stuff that the bag had disgorged. Then she pounced on a brown padded envelope.

'What have we here?' she laughed.

'Give that back!' Emily lunged for the envelope but Lauren dodged with a neat side-step. She ripped the envelope open with her teeth and pulled out a small plastic box. She flipped the box open, slid out an unlabelled black cassette tape and waved it at Ronnie, who was wedged halfway out of the laundry crate, clutching his ribs. 'Without this you have nothing! No proof that Nick was driving. No proof that Billy and Nick framed that Castelli guy!'

Emily made another grab for the tape, but she caught her foot in the strap of her bag and stumbled. By now Drift was back from hiding the iron pipe. He threw himself at Lauren's legs, barking and snarling, but she slipped out of reach behind a colossal, clanking, top-loader washing machine.

Lauren lifted the lid of the machine. Scott watched in horror, unable to move in case Billy struggled free, as she dropped the tape into the washing machine, pushing it down under the twists of soapy bedding. She flinched at the hot water but there was a triumphant smile on her face as she looked up. 'Where's your proof now?' she crowed.

At that moment the door burst open and everything started to happen at once. Police officers and security guards streamed into the laundry. Detective Inspector Hassan shouted orders. Two police officers handcuffed Lauren and another two tackled Billy. Dr Obi and Nurse Redpath ran in and helped Ronnie Brandon down from the laundry cart.

Billy cursed.

Lauren spat, 'No proof!'

Scott dived for the washing machine, yanked open the lid and pulled out the cassette. Everyone turned to stare at the ribbon of tape dangling from the plastic casing, tangled and knotted and dripping with soap suds.

Scott slumped to his knees. After all they'd been through, their evidence had been washed clean away.

'Never mind, kids,' Ronnie said kindly as he was being loaded into a wheelchair. 'You gave it your best shot.'

Emily grinned at him. 'Exactly!' she said. 'Which is

why we made sure Lauren and Billy didn't get hold of *this*!' She fished in her jeans pocket and held up a small key.

'What's that?' Scott and Ronnie chorused.

'Why do you think Jack got here before me?' Emily asked. 'Jack came directly from the Grand Vista Hotel, but I made a detour. I stopped off at the train station and got myself a left luggage locker.' Emily paused and smiled at Lauren. 'If I'd *really* been trying to stop you dropping the tape in the washing machine, I wouldn't have "tripped over" my bag, and I'd have told Drift to corner you properly, not just bark at you a bit! We just wanted you to *think* we were trying to get the tape back so you wouldn't suspect it was a dummy!'

Scott stared down at the mangled tape spilling out of his hands like a pile of worms. 'Well, you had me fooled! So what's *this* tape, then?'

'It's a Teach-Yourself-Spanish tape,' Emily laughed. 'I bought it from the newsagent stand. It's a good thing that Carrickstowe Station is a bit behind the times. I didn't know you could even buy these old cassette tapes any more. I just ripped the labels off and stuffed it in the envelope.' She held out the key to D. I. Hassan. 'Locker number seventeen. You'll find a tape made by Ronnie Brandon thirty years ago. On it, Billy Riordan and Nick Dylan admit that Nick Dylan was driving the Splinter Planet tour bus in an accident in 1974 that killed three people. And they offer hush money to Ronnie to go along with their cover story that Chris Castelli was driving.'

D. I. Hassan took the key. Scott, Emily and Jack watched as the police and security guards led Billy Riordan and Lauren Wade out of the laundry.

Lauren held her head high and struggled against the police officers. Billy looked so crushed he didn't even have the energy to swear. His long hair hung down over his eyes, the black strands dotted with blobs of fire extinguisher foam and washing powder.

Scott held the mangled tape out to Jack. 'Did *you* know this wasn't the real thing?'

Jack grinned. 'That would be telling!'

But Emily nodded. 'I hate to admit it,' she said. 'But it was Jack's idea!'

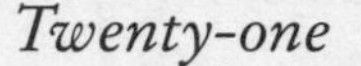

Twenty-one

Dreams Come True

It had been a rollercoaster kind of day, Scott thought, as he waited at the side of the main stage later that evening. It'd certainly had its low points – looking down the end of that iron pipe in the laundry to name but one – but since then, things had taken a massive turn for the better. He watched Emily's dad, Seth Wild, take the microphone and introduce the headline act of the Castle Key Music Festival.

The huge crowd cheered and whistled in excitement.

'Due to circumstances beyond our control,' Seth began, 'Splinter Planet will not be able to perform tonight.'

The cheering faded to a shocked silence.

'But don't worry!' Seth Wild shouted. 'We have a very special treat for you instead. Performing here, for one night only, I give you a new combined band – Panic Planet!' Seth turned to the wings and beckoned.

The singer and bass player from his old band, Panic Mode, jogged on to stage, smiling and waving. As soon as the crowd saw who it was, they went wild. Panic Mode hadn't played in public for years.

'And on drums,' Seth went on, 'Flak Petersen of Splinter Planet!' The lights went up to reveal Flak, dressed all in white, behind a huge silver drum kit, as ice-cool as ever. 'And, last but not least,' Seth announced, 'introducing, on lead guitar, our very own . . . '

Scott felt his heart ricochet around his rib cage as he waited for the name to be called out.

' . . . Scott Carter!'

Scott took a deep breath, gripped his guitar even tighter, and ran out onto the stage, blinking under the dazzling spotlights. Seth gave a signal and they launched into the opening chords of an old Splinter Planet hit, *Ready, Aim, Rock*. The crowd roared.

In the front row of the audience, Jack and Emily cheered and clapped until their hands tingled. Then they high-fived with the two men sitting next to them in their wheelchairs. On one side, Ronnie Brandon was sporting a huge cowboy hat and smiling happily. Dr Obi had agreed he was well enough to fly home to Texas – and to Rosa – the following morning. To the friends' huge excitement, Ronnie had promised that as soon as he was fully recovered, he'd fly them all out to Texas to stay on his ranch as a reward for saving his life!

Technically, Jack thought, *we saved Ronnie's life twice – once at Keyhole Cove and then again in the hospital laundry – so perhaps we're due* two *trips to Texas.* But he decided to let it pass. He didn't want to sound greedy, after all!

On the other side, Harry Stiles, his frail frame bundled up in mountains of blankets, nodded his head in time to the beat. 'Don't you go overdoing it again, Dad!' the plump woman behind the wheelchair said. 'We want you back home again soon!' She smiled at Jack. 'I don't know what medicine they've been giving him, but he seems chirpier than he's been in a long time!'

Harry winked at Jack and offered him a wine gum. 'Rock 'n' roll does you good!' the old man chortled.

Emily glanced down to check that Drift wasn't distressed by all the noise. He'd looked so downcast at the idea of being left alone at The Lighthouse that she'd found him a pair of earmuffs and brought him along to the concert. Now he was tucked up in the blankets on Harry's lap. Good old Drift! If he hadn't jumped down from Scott's bike to meet her as soon as she'd arrived at the hospital after her detour to the station, and then used his super-sensitive nose to follow the boys' trail straight to the laundry, Emily knew she probably wouldn't have got there in time to stop Billy Riordan.

She guessed D. I. Hassan had found the real tape in the left-luggage locker by now. She glanced across at Jack bouncing up and down to the beat. She'd been so furious with him after the climbing-out-of-the-window episode. But, then, as they were leaving the Grand Vista on their bikes, he'd suddenly come up with the brilliant idea of switching the tapes and taking a dummy to the hospital to dupe Lauren and Billy. How could she be angry after that stroke of genius?

Jack seemed to read her thoughts.

'You still planning to kill me then?' he shouted over the music.

Emily smiled. 'Yeah. I was thinking of doing it by throwing a sheet at you!'

Jack laughed. 'Good luck with that!'

Emily looked back at the stage. Scott was playing a solo now. She turned and grinned at Jack. 'Do you think he'll stop wanting to know us now that he's a rock star?'

'Only if we're lucky!' Jack joked.

Emily laughed, but she was half serious too. Operation Drowning Man had taught her that fame and fortune could do strange things to people. Just look at Nick Dylan and Billy Riordan. They'd been Ronnie's friends once. *But at least Nick has finally done the right thing,* she thought. He'd released a statement officially confirming that he, not Chris, had been driving the tour bus when the crash happened. He'd even promised to set up a charity in Chris Castelli's name.

Jack watched as Scott strutted around the stage, the crowd hanging on every chord. *Yeah,* he thought, *Scott might be a decent guitarist, but he's still only my brother!* 'And anyway,' he said, rolling his eyes at Emily. 'If Scott ever starts to get any big ideas, I know exactly how to bring him back to down to earth.' He handed Emily his phone. 'I'll just threaten to go public with this photo!'

Emily looked at the picture. It showed Scott standing on the beach at Keyhole Cove, at the precise moment that Emily's foot had made contact with his wrist. His mouth hung open as he gawped at the banana flying out of his hand. Everything about it was the exact opposite of cool.

'Yeah, that ought to do it,' Emily laughed.

But up on the stage Scott was having the time of his life. His last gig – with his band, the Banners – had been for twenty of his friends in the school hall. Now he was playing alongside a line-up of some of the best rock musicians in the world, in front of an adoring crowd of thousands. It didn't get any better than this!

Behind him, the ancient stone towers of the castle were splashed with a swirling rainbow of blue and green and pink lights. He looked out across the crowd, an ocean of faces as far as he could see. At the front, Ronnie Brandon and Harry Stiles were waving from their wheelchairs. Emily's mum was dancing. Even Old Bob and Aunt Kate were there! Jack and Emily looked up from giggling about something, and gave him a big thumbs-up.

Scott's dreams were all coming true.

It could only happen in Castle Key!

Don't miss the next exciting mystery
in the *Adventure Island* series

THE MYSTERY OF THE
SMUGGLERS' WRECK

Available June 2012!

Read on for a special preview of the first chapter.

One

The Wreck of the *Mermaid*

'That's where the *Mermaid* ran aground.'

Emily Wild pointed out across the bay towards Pirate Cove.

Jack took the binoculars and focused on the jagged rocks jutting up from the water, rocketing the waves into fountains of white spray.

Jack and his older brother Scott had only received Emily's text message (*New guest. V.v. interesting*) half an hour ago, but they'd sprinted all the way from Stone Cottage, where they were staying with their Great-aunt Kate for the Easter holidays. Emily never gave much away in a text (in case her phone fell into enemy hands, she claimed) but the boys knew her well enough to know that *v.v. interesting* had to be something good.

Now they were all sitting on the rocks below the old red and white lighthouse, which Emily's parents ran as a Bed and Breakfast, along with Emily's little dog Drift, of course. A young man with dark, closely cropped hair and light brown skin stretched over angular cheekbones and a square jaw was waging war with a large map; every time he unfolded another section, a wilful sea breeze flipped it up over his head.

'This is Joe Gordon,' Emily said. 'He checked in at The Lighthouse this morning.'

'Hi there!' Joe peeled the flapping map from his face and waved.

'Joe is going to be diving down to the shipwreck.' Emily scooped up a handful of stones and weighted the map down on a flat rock. Drift thought this was a great game. He began picking up pebbles in his jaws and dropping them on the map.

'So, you're exploring the *Mermaid* for your research?' Scott asked. Scott and Jack's dad, Leo Carter, was an archaeologist, so they were used to people trekking off to far-flung locations to unearth bits of ancient history.

But Scott couldn't help feeling a bit disappointed. Since they'd started coming to Castle Key last summer, the guests at The Lighthouse had included an ex-SAS stunt man, a glamorous international art thief and a group of legendary rock stars. Joe Gordon seemed a nice enough guy, but a *historian* wasn't exactly in the same league – even if he was wearing the coolest pair of trainers Scott had seen in a long time.

But Joe Gordon shook his head. 'No, it's not research exactly, I'm—'

'Joe's just started a diving company that recovers valuable cargo from shipwrecks,' Emily interrupted.

Scott was impressed. 'A *professional treasure-hunter*?'

'You mean that's actually a *job*?' Jack asked in disbelief. 'How come nobody mentioned that one at our last school careers day?'

Joe laughed. 'We've been trying to keep it a secret for years!'

'So what do you think you'll find down there?' Scott nudged aside a pile of Drift's stones and studied the map. Joe had marked the location of the wreck in red pen.

Joe rubbed his chin. 'Well, the *Mermaid's* been down there over two hundred years. She sank in—'

'1779,' Emily chipped in.

'That's right. She was a big cutter belonging to—'

'Thomas Pendragon,' Emily interrupted again. 'He was the owner of Pendragon Manor at the time.'

'Exactly,' Joe said. 'A wealthy landowner. But he was also a well-known—'

'Smuggler!' Emily breathed, her eyes shining with delight.

Joe Gordon turned to the boys and grinned. 'Is she always like this?'

Scott and Jack both nodded. 'Yeah.'

'Like *what*?' Emily interrupted.

Scott, Jack and Joe Gordon laughed.

'You haven't let Joe finish a single sentence, Em,' Scott explained.

Jack came to Emily's defence. 'She can't help it. Smuggling is one of Emily's favourite subjects. Along with espionage and criminal investigation. She's totally obsessed.'

'I am *not* obsessed!' Emily protested, raking tresses of long conker-brown hair out of her eyes. She was seriously considering giving both Scott and Jack a hefty shove. But she stopped herself. For a start, they might fall off the rocks into the sea. *And maybe they have a point,* she thought reluctantly. *I suppose I might have been bulldozing Joe a bit.* 'OK, I promise I won't butt in any more!' She laughed and mimed a lip-zipping action.

Joe Gordon smiled. 'It's OK. I don't blame you for being interested. The history of smuggling in Cornwall is fascinating. It was big business in the eighteenth century. Brandy, silver, tobacco, tea, silks . . . Most people round here were involved one way or another. It was one of the few ways to make a living.'

'And everyone hated the customs men who came to collect the taxes,' Emily added. Then she clapped her hand over her mouth. 'Oops, I'm doing it again!'

'That's alright. You go for it,' Joe said with a grin. 'You obviously know your stuff.'

'The inlets near Pirate Cove, and further west around Keyhole Cove, were perfect places to land the smuggled goods,' Emily explained, 'because only local sailors knew how to navigate the treacherous rocks. Customs boats wouldn't dare approach.'

'Tell me about it!' Jack laughed, remembering their own recent escapades saving a drowning man in Keyhole Cove. Those rocks were lethal.

'So how come the *Mermaid* ran aground if the smugglers knew their way around?' Scott asked, as logical as ever.

'Thomas Pendragon was betrayed!' Emily said dramatically. She remembered the story well. Old Bob the fisherman had told it to her many a time. 'One of the servants at Pendragon Manor had been accused of stealing from the house, so she decided to get her revenge. She found out when the *Mermaid* would next be sailing back from France running a cargo of contraband, and she tipped off the customs men. They overpowered the smugglers' landing party – the men who were waiting to help unload – and then lay in wait at Pirate Cove to catch the smugglers as they came ashore. But one of Pendragon's men on the island heard about the ambush plan and lit a fire on the cliff near the castle to warn him.'

Jack followed Emily's gaze up to the ruined castle high on the cliff top. He could almost see the beacon burning. 'So what happened?'

'Pendragon tried to retreat but it was too late. The customs men fired on them from land and from small boats,' Emily went on. 'In all the confusion, the *Mermaid* hit the rocks and sank. All hands – including Pendragon – were drowned.'

'Wow!' Jack whistled. 'Cool story.'

He turned to Joe Gordon. 'And now you're going to salvage all the smuggled cargo from the wreck?' His imagination was running on turbo power, conjuring up an underwater Aladdin's cave of gold ingots and glittering jewels.

Joe shook his head. 'Unfortunately, there's not much left down there. There've been lots of dives over the years and anything valuable has been taken already. No, I'm looking for the body of Thomas Pendragon.'

Scott frowned. 'Surely it's just a skeleton?'

'It's what the skeleton's *wearing* that I'm interested in,' Joe said.

Jack was puzzled. 'But won't all the cloth have rotted into fish food by now?'

'I'm not after his *clothes*,' Joe explained. 'The company

that now own the Pendragon Estate contacted me a few weeks ago. Their lawyers found an old letter in the library at the manor. It's from Thomas Pendragon to his son. It mentions a special compass with some kind of map or code engraved into the brass lid, revealing the secret hiding place where Pendragon and other smugglers stashed their contraband before selling it on. To this day, it's never been found.'

Secret hiding place! The thrilling words sent a shiver down Jack's spine. This story just kept getting better. 'So you're going to find the compass and *then* find the treasure?'

'That's the plan. The new owners of the Pendragon Estate have hired me to try to recover the compass for them. In the old letter, Pendragon told his son that he always wore the compass on a chain around his neck.'

Suddenly Scott noticed that they'd been talking about smuggling for two whole minutes and Emily hadn't interrupted once! 'Are you alright, Em?' he asked.

'Hm? What?' Emily murmured. She'd hardly heard Scott's question. She was too busy gazing out towards Pirate Cove. Somewhere, far beneath those cold, deep waters, the wreck of the *Mermaid* had lain silent for hundreds of years, along with her ghostly skeleton crew and the key to a secret hoard of forgotten treasures! An idea was unfolding in Emily's mind – an idea so magical she hardly dared put it into words.

Wouldn't it be the most amazing adventure ever to be the one to find the Pendragon compass?

When she finally spoke, Emily's voice was barely more than a whisper. 'You couldn't take me down to the wreck, could you?'